How Can I Help You

Also by Laura Sims

FICTION

Looker

POETRY

Staying Alive

My God Is This a Man

Stranger

Practice, Restraint

NONFICTION

Fare Forward: Letters from David Markson

How Can
I Help You

Laura Sims

G. P. PUTNAM'S SONS · NEW YORK

PUTNAM
— EST. 1838 —

G. P. PUTNAM'S SONS
Publishers Since 1838
An imprint of Penguin Random House LLC
penguinrandomhouse.com

Library of Congress Cataloging-in-Publication Data
Names: Sims, Laura, 1973– author.
Title: How can I help you / Laura Sims.
Description: New York: G. P. Putnam's Sons, 2023.
Identifiers: LCCN 2023018916 (print) | LCCN 2023018917 (ebook) |
ISBN 9780593543702 (hardcover) | ISBN 9780593543726 (ebook)
Subjects: LCGFT: Thrillers (Fiction) | Novels.
Classification: LCC PS3619.I565 H69 2023 (print) | LCC PS3619.I565
(ebook) | DDC 813/.6—dc23/eng/20230425
LC record available at https://lccn.loc.gov/2023018916
LC ebook record available at https://lccn.loc.gov/2023018917

Printed in the United States of America
1st Printing

Book design by Elke Sigal

For Mona and her profanely inspiring advice

In the library, time is dammed up—not just stopped but saved. The library is a gathering pool of narratives and of the people who come to find them. It is where we can glimpse immortality; in the library, we can live forever.

—Susan Orlean, *The Library Book*

Who has not asked himself at some time or other: am I a monster or is this what it means to be a person?

—Clarice Lispector, *The Hour of the Star*

It is madness to write things down.

—Elizabeth Bowen, *The Death of the Heart*

How Can I Help You

I.

Working Like the Devil

MARGO

The moment I walked through the front door, I knew. That deep, abiding quiet, and the sense that the outside world couldn't reach me here. I was like someone chased by demons across the threshold of a church, stepping into the library that first time. I could have turned around, right there at the door, and stuck my tongue out at the world.

Can't catch me.

I didn't do it, and besides, the world wasn't watching. Couldn't find me anyway, could it? I'd already changed my hair and makeup, my clothes, my voice, and even the way I walked. I'd changed my name, too. I'd been Jane but I was Margo now. I liked Margo. Jane would have turned and stuck her tongue out, but Margo never would. No, Margo simply stood in the vestibule, shoulders back and head held high like a queen.

I hadn't spent much time in libraries before then. It was quiet as a nighttime ICU ward—maybe quieter, without all the noise that goes with slow dying: the *whoosh* of respirators, the mechanical beeps of infusion pumps. I stared up at the high, vaulted ceiling and around at the egg-white walls, then sat down at one of the public computers. I checked the want ads and saw one for circulation clerk right there at the Carlyle Public Library. I toiled over a cover letter and résumé for an hour or so, then handed them in at the desk. "I was so happy to see this job come up," I said to the stout, red-haired woman there. She seemed managerial, but I learned later that Liz was just a regular staff member. "I can't imagine a more peaceful work environment," I went on, waving my arm around. She chuckled a bit, as if I'd said something funny. But from what I could tell, the library was just that: quiet, anonymous, orderly, and sane. From the grandness of the old building to the way the light slanted through the high windows that afternoon, I knew I'd landed in a cozy, carpeted, outdated vault, and I loved it on sight. The job was what I wanted, too: helping people. Not the way I'd helped them before, at the hospital, but still. I would be serving others. When I'd glanced around at the careworn souls sitting at the monitors that day, I'd known there would be plenty of work for me here, plenty of helping to do.

Liz and I struck up a conversation. I told her how long I'd been in town, how much I was enjoying the weekend farmers' market—though I hadn't even been—and the birdsong outside my window every morning. She seemed like the bird-watching type. I told her I'd seen cardinals, wrens, and woodpeckers, though the only birds I'd really seen were the pigeons in the parking lot of my Soviet-era apartment complex, pecking at the ground. I told her a tale about moving from Indianapolis, where all I could hear was the roaring river of cars. I told her I'd hated it, hated the overrated canal walk and the seedy downtown, and had moved for a much-needed change. Liz and I were laughing like old friends before long, and she said she'd put in a good word for me.

And now here I am, two years later, checking out patrons' books, DVDs, and audiobooks, answering their questions about overdue fees with patient grace, policing the computers where I myself sat that first day, making sure the guy in the baseball hat who comes in on Fridays doesn't watch porn while he's pretending to job-search. I understand now why Liz chuckled that first day; the library *is* peaceful, on the whole, but disturbances happen. Patrons shout into their cell phones, throw tantrums over lost books, or hide, half-naked, in hidden corners of the stacks. I'm never bored here—the way I thought I might be when I first arrived.

I sneak up behind Friday Guy, as we've come to call him, and lean right over his shoulder so my breath is hot on his neck. "Hey," I say. He jumps and fumbles, tries to click screens to cover up the giant tits I just saw bouncing before my eyes. Then he looks up, red-faced. Sweating, even in the cold of the main room. "You know the rules," I say, drawing up to my full height. "Yes, ma'am." I feel a deep tickle when he calls me ma'am and obeys me like a scolded dog. "I'm watching you," I tell him. "Yes, ma'am." He blinks up at me with his sad gray eyes. After a long pause, I walk away.

Liz and the younger clerk, Nasrin, watch me return to the desk, triumphant. "You're amazing," Nasrin says, shaking her head in wonder. I just shrug. "You should have seen the double-Ds he was ogling today," I say, lifting my eyebrows. Nasrin covers her mouth as we all stand there, the two of them giggling like children. I don't even bother being discreet—I'm laughing my deep laugh when Friday Guy slinks past the desk, still red-faced, carrying plastic bags full of loose papers as usual. Every time I think: *He won't come back. He'll find some other unsuspecting branch, one without a Margo.* But every Friday, he's there, eyeing those tits, waiting for me to catch him. I guess he likes the game of it.

I like the game of it, too. My nipples, tucked inside my padded bra, get hard every time we perform our little ritual. It isn't like my hospital days, but it's better than nothing.

I had to earn this swagger, though. I didn't start out swishing through the aisles, expertly managing Friday Guy and others. When I first started, I was clueless, fumbling, and forgetful. I made rushed notes on a legal pad, things like:

- DO NOT renew patrons' computer time more than once, for more than an hour
- Password for scanner is: SCANTHIS
- Checkout forms for hot spots and tablets in drawer to my right
- Must take elderly/infirm ~~patients~~ patrons downstairs in elevator with smallest key on ring
- Call the non-emergency police number for someone acting out but not dangerous
- Call 911 for someone dangerous to himself or others

The last two items tickled me, but I'd held my face still as Yvonne, our director, explained what could differentiate one situation from another: realistic threats of violence, a weapon suggested or in sight, crazed appearance or language. She used the male pronoun for every scenario she described, so I wrote it down: *he, he.* And she was right, for the most part; the only times I've punched the numbers 911 into the phone, it's been for men. Men can never keep their violence to themselves.

But incidents like those were and are rare, though even ordinary scenarios flustered me back then. When someone approached the desk without books in hand, it meant they had a question, one I wasn't sure I could answer. I tried to draw on my nursing expertise, but a nurse isn't much good in a library. And I wasn't supposed to be a nurse, of course; I was supposed to be an "experienced library assistant," like my résumé said. So I bluffed my way through as best as I could, and if Liz, Nasrin, or Yvonne caught me in a slip, I'd just say that my last library had different systems for everything. They accepted my ignorance—welcomed it, even. They were endlessly forgiving and kind. Quick to swoop in and rescue me from disgruntled patrons, though most of the patrons were patient with me, too, telling me I had a beautiful smile or an infectious laugh even when I was failing to help them. They used my name when they learned it, and that made me feel seen. Well, "seen" in the safest way possible; they saw me as Margo, or Ms. Finch—not as Jane, of course. Some days I felt the way I had in my earliest nursing days—when my uniform was a crisp, bright blue and I'd swell with pride at the slightest praise. For those first few weeks at the library, I let myself be as ignorant and swaddled as an infant; it felt like floating in a nice, hot bath.

I've always believed in the restorative properties of baths—for my patients and myself. I've bathed many a human body in distress and seen the wonders that steam and hot water can work. Even when the file said "sponge bath only" I would defy it and fully bathe the poor soul. They needed it, didn't they? And I was strong enough to handle their bodies on my own. It was a bit of a struggle, but we all need to be immersed in water, cleansed and petted by human hands. A sponge bath just doesn't cut it. Though I would limit myself to sponge baths if I were under close observation, as I often was in the final days at one hospital after another. I would start off cheerful, energetic, everyone's favorite new colleague. Eventually, though, they'd start to look at me too long. Whisper when I left the room. They would ask me things like, *What were you doing in Mr. Hammerson's room? Why have you checked this and that out from the medicine supply? Why haven't you noted here and there what you've done in the file?*

They also interfered with my patients' baths—but they couldn't interfere with my own. Back at home, I'd close my eyes in the tub and sweat out the rancor and suspicion they piled on me, from one place to the next. Sacred Heart. Green Grove. Union Community. Highland Medical. Spring Hill. Each one started as a paradise—like the names suggest—but ended in quiet fury and disgrace.

My fury; *their* disgrace, I remind myself.

But Margo tries not to linger in the past. It does her no

good. She was wronged; she moved on. Movement is key, I've found. To always be moving, wherever I am—even in circles sometimes.

I sweep by the computer aisle whenever I can. Push in the empty chairs with my hip and straighten the stacks of notepaper and tiny pencils arranged near each station. As I make my rounds today, a rumpled old man leans back and calls me over, his sad eyes brimming with almost-death, his need to be held—and possibly bathed—tugging fiercely at my insides.

"Miss, can you help?" he asks. When I reach him, I put my face close to his and look at his screen. I smell his sour breath, the unwashed scent of his clothes, and don't falter for a second. I inhale deeply through my nose so he'll know I'm not repulsed one bit. Not even one tiny bit. "The screen froze," he says. I push a button here and there, toggle the mouse back and forth, then sigh. "We've got to shut this thing down and start it back up," I tell him. "Sometimes that's all it takes. Don't you worry." I make the screen go black. Then I punch the power button and bring it back to life. His face lights up like he's seen the workings of a god. "Thank you, miss." "Of course." I hold him with my eyes, probing those pathetic depths, then I let him go.

Do I feel a twinge of frustration?

I do.

Those eyes, begging me for help. I *want* to help—the way I used to. But I left the last hospital in the dust, and that's how it should be. No—*should be* doesn't matter. That's *how it is*. Margo doesn't live in some imaginary world where Jane goes on doing her rounds. Margo lives in the real world: the library. To prove it, I grab a stack of books to reshelve, tell Nasrin I'll be back. But when I've found my rhythm—locating each book's spot, sliding it into place—the hospital sneaks back, seeps into me: the peaceful night-shift realm I used to inhabit amid the honeycomb cells of the ICU. I would roam back and forth, back and forth, practically gliding on those smooth, polished floors, checking pulses here and there, resting my warm hand on a sleepy head. Leaning down to feel a faint breath on my cheek, my lips.

But chaos could erupt from the heart of this quiet, too; suddenly I'd find myself standing by a patient's bedside as commotion descended: hurried footsteps, shouted directions. I stayed calm, soothing the forehead or hands of a struggling one, shushing them gently, steadily handing this or that to the doctor while keeping my eyes locked on the terrified eyes. I'd show them my shining face and my beatific smile and they clung to it, hung their souls onto it, and sometimes they gripped my arms with their wasted claws and literally held me, and I let them. They needed me. I was their living, breathing saint: their nurse. Even if I couldn't save them. Even if, at that point, no one could.

"The ones that die are the lucky ones," I once said to Donna, the head nurse I considered a friend—a close friend, the closest friend I'd ever had. I said it right after an "untimely death," one that had rattled everyone—even the patient's neglectful family. *They said she was doing okay two days ago*, her eldest son choked out through tears. From what I'd seen and from what the day nurses said, he'd only visited twice, and both times he'd sat in the corner staring blankly at game shows on the hospital TV. He didn't kiss her brow or talk lovingly to her the way I always did, in the quiet of night. I saw how lost she was, how alone. I saw what she needed in the pools of her eyes when they stared up at me in the muted light.

I hadn't meant to say what I said to Donna out loud, but I had, and there was no taking it back. A small part of me thought she might agree, but she stared. "Really? You really think that, Jane?" she asked. Like she'd never considered it herself. Like she hadn't seen how they shuttled so many sad, crippled, hurting souls from the ICU out through the main doors into cruel sunshine and wished them well, sent off to linger alone in some shadowed room until time finished them. They may as well have given them a great shove into the busy parking lot and left them wherever they fell. The untimely-death woman didn't appear to fit that mold—not to a casual observer like Donna—but I'd witnessed the woman's suffering firsthand. Maybe she would have gone home and recovered, but to what end? There were crueler fates than a quick death. But Donna didn't get it, or couldn't stomach it, or just couldn't admit the truth of it to herself, so I told her I was kidding and left it at that. She opened her mouth to say something more but then closed it and shifted her eyes away. Usually, Donna and I could chuckle over anything. But that time she pursed her lips and took a sip of tea.

Through the years, I've learned to be careful. Careful what you say and to whom, careful how you carry yourself at all times. I carried myself regally on my rounds, and then let my hair down and laughed hysterically in the break room. Always had a tale ready to cheer up my fellow nurses. Made-up stories of my love life, raunchy jokes, lies and more lies. Sometimes they laughed until they cried. "Jolly Jane," they said, shaking their heads and wiping their eyes. "Tell us another one. No—don't!"

"Did I tell you about the time my ex-husband lit his own pants on fire?"

"The old man in 307 waved me over just now, beckoned me close, and then he squeezed my tits like two melons! Dropped right back to sleep after that, like he'd had his snack and was satisfied."

"That raving homeless woman who was in the other night kept telling me she could turn her piss into wine! I asked her to bring me a cup."

I'd have the whole room rapt or in stitches. Nurses needed help, too—they were tired and traumatized by all they'd had to touch, see, smell, and do. They left the break room feeling renewed; I saw to that. I was holding the hospital—whichever one it was at the time—up and afloat in the palm of my hand. And they knew it, every one of them knew it, but it didn't stop them from chasing me out, pitchforks in hand.

Closing my eyes for a moment, I relish having escaped, having found my way to the library. Late Friday afternoons tend to be quiet, but I can still drift on the tide of familiar sounds: the soft clatter of fingers across keyboards, the thud of books landing in the return slot, the ruffling of pages, the mechanical *whoosh* as the front door opens and closes, sealing us inside. Standing here, swaying a little, I feel as relaxed as I might after a long vacation. I never felt this way at any hospital; it was a great burden, you know, helping so many for so long. Jane loved it, but it hardened her. Margo is softer, and less hurried, too, in her dealings with patients. Patrons. *Patrons.* It shouldn't matter what we call them, really; they're the same in the end. *Patrons* will land in hospital beds at one point or other—for sickness, for surgery, for death. I can't touch them the way I touched *patients*, though; I might pat someone on the hand or back, or possibly squeeze an arm, but that's as far as it goes. Sometimes I miss the heft and smell of flesh other than my own, the rigors of my practice as a nurse, but I tell myself how lucky I am, to be a librarian.

Sticklers would say I'm *not* a librarian—I have no official degree. Liz lords it over me sometimes, though it's not as if patrons know the difference. To them I'm *Ms. Finch, the librarian.* I even bought reading glasses that hang on a beaded chain around my neck. I love raising them to my eyes to peer down at the book title a patron has written down, or at the monitor of a troublesome computer. "Thank you, Ms. Finch," the patrons always say, with some reverence, when I'm wearing my glasses. Instant gravitas.

When the glasses are off, though, I'm quick to laugh. Sometimes my laugh rings out in the quiet and rattles a patron or two, who look up, as if *they* would admonish *me.* But they can't—libraries now allow laughter. And some level of noise. This took some getting used to at first, when I would circulate and shush the teens in their after-school corner of the adult floor. They chose the spot where outdated technology books met crumbling old biographies, but I sought them out. They would blink up at me as if I were an indiscriminate mass instead of a woman who stood nearly six feet tall, towering over them, staring. They'd pause for just a moment, then resume chatting. Yvonne pulled me aside one day and explained: "The library is a community center now. It's a gathering place. We want people to come together and, yes, talk, if they want to. We want young people to come here and hang out. If they grow up in the library, they'll value it later, see?"

Sounded desperate to me, grasping. But Margo smiled and nodded.

I'm not interested in the young anyway, so it was easy to leave them be. Throbbing with health as they are, insolent and arrogant in their certainty of immortal life. Give them twenty or thirty more years, let them taste a bit of failure, loss, sickness, uncertainty, and death, and then wheel them into my room; I'll care for them without an ounce of resentment. They'll long to hear my rubber soles squeaking down the hall and look for my hand bearing a tiny paper cup of pills or a needle full of merciful relief. They'll let me turn their bodies on the bed, checking for sores, scanning the bedpan to see what they've done, and if they've done something, I'll say, "Good girl" or "Good boy," and they'll glow with pride as I tidy them up, put their sheets right, push a stray hair out of their eyes, change the channel for them if their hands are too weak to hold the remote. They'll thank me then—with trembling chins and bright wet eyes.

I mean they *would* thank me. They *would*.

♦ ♦ ♦

One day, during my first year here, Liz asked, out of nowhere, "Do you read?" with that sharpness to her voice that told me it would bother her if I said no. So I told her, "Of course," and went on pulling books from the shelves, examining their publication dates and the condition they were in. I clenched, waiting for her follow-up questions: *Who's your favorite author? What's the best book you've read lately?* But they didn't come. I was relieved but insulted, too. We went on weeding. I had a small pile of books beside me I thought should be pulled from the collection; Liz's pile was larger. Was that because she was a reader and had some secret knowledge I wasn't privy to? I told myself I didn't care. The truth is I don't read; when I've tried to here and there, it's been too unsettling, reading someone else's thoughts and feelings in fine print. I have enough of a time dealing with my own thoughts and feelings—why should I take on someone else's, too? Also, I'm far too busy—or I was. When I worked as a nurse, I'd go home, eat, and fall into a deep sleep. It isn't like that now, but I still have no desire to read. Readers aren't doers, are they? And wherever I've been, whether Jane or Margo— or that other one, the first one—I've always been a doer.

Even so, I couldn't stop hearing Liz's question: *Do you read?* As if it were a crime to work in a library and not go on and on about books the way she and Nasrin did. I spent my lunch hour that day scanning the fiction shelves, hoping to show up back at the desk with a novel or two in hand.

Wouldn't that have thrown her? I would have been casual about it, would have slid them into my bag like it was something I did all the time. But as I stared at a row of books by authors with last names beginning with V, I couldn't make heads or tails of any of them. *Two Trains Running* by Andrew Vachss, *Find Me* by Laura van den Berg, *Call Me Zebra* by Azareen Van der Vliet Oloomi, *The Secret of Raven Point* by Jennifer Vanderbes, *Acceptance* by Jeff VanderMeer . . . the names and titles started to blur. I reached up and plucked *Find Me* from the shelf at random, flipped through to the first lines: "Things I will never forget—my name, my made-up birthday . . . The dark of the hospital at night. My mother's face, when she was young." I slammed the book shut. I felt like someone had snuck up behind me, tapped my shoulder, and said my original name out loud. I put the book back, enjoying the motion of that: of putting it back, of making sure the spine was lined up with the others beside it. *That* gave me pleasure, just the way it always gave me pleasure to arrange the medicine on shelves in the hospital supply room. When they'd ask me, "What were you doing in there for so long?" I'd say, "I was straightening the shelves—what a mess!" And I wasn't lying, exactly—I always left things neater than they'd been before. My questioners would smile, nod their heads, mutter thanks. By the end, though, they'd have a cold look in their eyes when they saw me leaving the supply room.

Things I will never forget: that cold look in their eyes.

At some point, the hospital director would call me into their office and hand me a referral letter. Grimly, as if it pained them to do it. Jane took the letter with pride, like it was something she'd asked for, and went on to the next place, and the next—until Spring Hill, where it ended.

Which brought me here, among the books. I didn't have to read them to know how to care for them, no matter what Liz said; I certainly didn't need to read to know how to care for the people who wanted them. While Liz sat there, perusing the books, or the library's catalog of books, or the Internet's lists of books, I was out on the floor, working like the devil: sanitizing computer workstations, straightening flyers for the next Friends of the Library jewelry sale, and giving patrons whatever help they needed, whatever company they wanted. *That*, in my view, was being a librarian: being a *doer*.

"You never stop," Nasrin said once, admiringly.

"That's because I can't," I replied, laughing.

And it's true: Instead of one lap around the public computers, I do three. And if the glass panes on the front door are looking grimy, I grab the 409 and a roll of paper towels. "You don't need to do that," Yvonne said once, touching me gently on the arm as I scrubbed. "Oh, it's all right," I said, smiling back at her. "But our cleaning crew will do that," she explained. I already knew. She thought it was beneath me, I guess, to be cleaning the windows. But I've also found that it's better to have a task than to circle like an anxious cat.

Lately I *have* been anxious. Even with work filling my days, I've felt the edge of dread creep in. Is it the sudden onset of fall? The early dark? *Is that all that's bugging you, Margo?* I can't think what else, except that I've been here now for over two years, and that's longer than I stayed at any one of my hospitals. Maybe that's all that's making me restless and moody, a little bit bored.

Perhaps. Or maybe it's something coming down the pipe. Something I can't see yet, though I sometimes find myself staring into space, toward the front door.

MARGO

I'm circling today, but with purpose. A week has passed and it's Friday again. Friday Guy has taken up his spot and waits for me—though not for long. The first time I pass, he's looking at a jobs list. The second time, he's browsing hunting knives. I hang back, feeling the atmosphere thicken. The third time—sure enough—I get a partial glimpse of plump breasts, the curve of a hip. He's thrown the knife site up for cover—but he hasn't done a good job. I think he must have *meant* to do a bad job.

"You're scum," I lean down and whisper in his ear.

It's not what I meant to say—or what I'm supposed to say—but it's out now, isn't it? I can't see Friday Guy's face but I can tell I've rattled him. I sniff at his neck, catching a whiff of body odor and stale breath. "You stink," I say in my softest voice. "Don't come here again without bathing first." I straighten up slowly. "Yes, ma'am," he says, staring, red-faced, as I walk away.

"What did you say to him?" Liz asks, eyebrows raised. Nasrin is there, too, poised on the verge of laughter. I could lead her right over the brim, but instead I play it cool. "I told him the same thing I always do. 'You know the rules,'" I say, shrugging. Liz looks dubious. "He seemed scared," she says, but I don't waver. "I thought he looked the way he always does, personally. And I'm the only one who sees him up close." Liz makes a sound in the back of her throat while Nasrin watches the two of us, giving me her warm smile. But it falters a bit, doesn't it? She turns from me more quickly than usual. There will be no chuckling together today, no gleeful camaraderie. I feel that sinking in my stomach that I've felt so many times before. At the hospitals—not here. But I've done nothing wrong and this isn't the hospital, is it? It's the library. The *library*. The word alone soothes me.

The day ends the way it always does: quietly. After shooing out the last patrons, we turn out the overhead lights, gather our sweaters off the backs of our chairs, and lock the door behind us. I'm the only one who walks instead of drives. Because sidewalks are scarce, I have to trudge home through grass with cars whizzing by. Still, I find it invigorating after the long workday. In twenty-five minutes, I see the faded concrete block of my apartment building ahead of me. Soon I'm climbing the blue metal staircase to number 39, dropping my bag by the door once I'm inside, and running a hot bath. I don't feel the urgency I felt during my nursing days, when I would come home exhausted and gritty, or sometimes coated in filth. The closest I get to filth now is peering over Friday Guy's shoulder once a week. But still I come home, strip down, and lower myself into a tub of scalding water. There's a spasm of pain at first, but soon my mind goes blank, my limbs and muscles loosen; my eyes focus hazily on the rise of my belly, or my reddening knees beyond it, jutting out of the water. I drift and dream. Everything that came before—my seasonal unease, my odd harshness toward Friday Guy, the tension with Liz and Nasrin—subsides into the water.

Afterward, I wrap my rosy pink self in my favorite robe, one that once belonged to a patient. She was just my size, and it was soft and baby blue: my favorite color. I wind my hair in a towel and then I make myself a simple dish of pasta with garlic, cream sauce, spinach, and white beans. Holding my bowl, I scan the news on my old beast of a computer. There was a whole flurry of stories about Jane when I first arrived in Carlyle. "Search for Fugitive Nurse Runs Dry." "'Nurse Jane' Disappears into Thin Air." I didn't *disappear*, though, as the fools must know. As if I'd dissolved right down to my atoms. No, I transformed. Emerged here, in a life they could never imagine. It was fun to chuckle over those stories in the safety of my new life, warm from the bath, tucked in my favorite chair. But the press has trickled down to almost nothing now. It doesn't bother me; it was only a diversion. And it's better, of course, if the news has died down. The world has moved on—so have I.

It took a long time, though, to move my body and soul out of night shift mode, and to shake off the terrors of the recent past. For weeks I woke from dreams of running through an unending labyrinth of hospital halls. I'd wake sweating, eyes staring around my strange new room in the dark. Where was I? Prison? *No, no*, I'd whisper to Jane. *Not prison. A new life.* Jane's heart went on beating like a wild animal's, though: *Let me out. Let me out. Let me out.*

But soon enough we adapted. Now I turn in early every night, wake at five. I stretch my arms up over my head, wiggle my fingers and toes, and smile to myself at the thought of a new day. This time it's Saturday. A free day. I'll go about my shopping and chores with a light heart and smiles for everyone.

♦ ♦ ♦

When Monday arrives and a woman walks through our door, sending a gust of early fall breeze my way, I feel a tickle of unease. She looks around, sniffing the air like she's smelled something bad, and then she sees me and walks toward the circulation desk. She's tall—almost as tall as I am—but slim, flat-chested, with olive-toned skin. She has glossy black shoulder-length hair and wide, dark eyes behind red-rimmed glasses. Like mine, I realize, touching my glasses where they hang around my neck. I see her white teeth flash behind her red lips when she smiles and think: *Donna*. She doesn't look like Donna at all—Donna was short, heavy, and huge boobed, with paper-white skin and wavy dirty-blond hair—but somehow this woman *is* Donna. Gives off the air of Donna. Donna, my old, dead friend. She isn't *really* dead, of course. I've looked her up on the hospital website: she's still there, still the head ICU nurse. She's not *here*, I remind myself, staring at the stranger dressed mostly in black. Donna never wore black.

"Hi, is Yvonne Matthews available?" she asks. Maybe she's a board member I haven't met. She's young for that, though. "Yes, just a moment. Who can I say—?" "Patricia," she says, drawing out the syllables. *Pa-tree-see-ah.* "Patricia Delmarco." I summon Yvonne, who greets her warmly, and the two walk back to Yvonne's office. I watch the door close as a patron approaches the desk. "My computer won't print," I hear them say, as if from a distance.

Yvonne and Pa-tree-see-ah are together for close to an hour. I imagine them back there, Yvonne talking, Patricia tilting her head to the right and holding Yvonne's gaze just the way Donna did. It was a trick she had of making you feel listened to, appreciated, cared for. I confided so many things to her—some of them true—with her green eyes fixed on me that way.

Nothing like the look she gave me that last day. The look that made me feel repugnant, despised. The look that chased me from my patient's room, down the hall, and out through the sliding glass doors.

Into sunlight. Into this new life, I remind myself. I take a deep breath. *That's not Donna back there. Don't be stupid, Margo.*

The slight clearing of a throat distracts me. Judy, a regular, has piled her stack of Nora Roberts books on the desk. She leans close to me and asks, "You want to hear a funny story?" I nod as if I have a choice. "I went to my hematologist on Monday, because my platelet count was high. The doctor said, 'I hate patients like you.'" I keep a fixed smile on my face, knowing what's coming next. "'Because there's nothing wrong with you!'" she finishes, triumphant, crowing. She stands there, somewhere in her eighties, hands twitching, eyelids drooping, strands of hair barely covering her scalp: exultant. "That's fantastic!" I respond, warming to her triumph, connecting with what must have been her fear, her anxiety, now washed away by a tide of relief—like my own, when I discovered the library. Her eyes start to tear as we beam at each other, and mine do, too. I pat Judy's hand and pass her the books. I liked the warm, bony feel of her hand. I wish I could have held it.

Before I know it, Yvonne and Pa-tree-see-ah are walking toward the door. I watch their backs: one tall and slim, one short and stout. They shake hands and say their good-byes.

There goes the stranger, back out into the world.

It's satisfying, watching her go. As the door shuts behind her, the same cool breeze wafts toward me that did when she arrived. It ruffles papers. I slap my hand down to still them.

Yvonne comes straight to the circ desk, swallowing a smile. "Well, that's our new reference librarian," she says, spreading her hands like she's just performed a magic trick. "I offered her the job, and she accepted." She looks as though she's won an unbelievable prize. She's grinning, her white teeth bright against her brown skin. Normally I love the sight of her dimples, but I'm too unnerved to relish them now. "Oh," I say, afraid of how I sound, how I'm holding my face. I remember, now, that we've had an ad up for a reference librarian for several months. The desk has sat empty for over twelve years, but Yvonne finally won approval from the board to fund the position. She was thrilled. But then the job search crawled along, with few qualified candidates, and we all just assumed the desk would stay empty. Now the Donna-like Pa-tree-see-ah will be sitting right across from me, separated only by carpet and air. "When does she start?" I ask as lightly as I can. "Next week. Just as soon as the board approves her—but they will. Now we'll finally have someone at the reference desk," Yvonne says with a sigh. We both stare at the empty desk—Yvonne with deep contentment, I with growing dread.

The reference desk has been the main floor's dumping ground for damaged books, old program flyers, and stacks of local papers for as long as I've been here, or longer. Looking over there, I can't help thinking how Patricia—however I feel about her—with her stylish dark clothes, her smooth and shining hair, can't possibly sit in that dusty pit. I tell Yvonne I'm going to straighten things up, and before long, I'm treading the carpet back and forth, back and forth, carrying arm-loads of damaged books down to the old stacks, where the most delicate and decrepit books are kept. I find several empty shelves and arrange the books there. Then I jog back upstairs to print a sign that says DAMAGED. I feel deadly efficient, like an OR nurse in the middle of surgery. And, like an OR nurse, I don't think. I just *do*.

By the end of an hour, I've recycled a small mountain of paper, cleared off most of the desk, and begun work on the main desk drawer. It's crammed with all sorts of odds and ends: loose, anonymous keys; several pairs of dice; rusty safety pins; bottle tops; and an ancient, broken stapler. Everything purposeless goes in the trash. I wipe out the inside of the drawer and fill Patricia's tray with scrap paper, a staple remover, Scotch tape, and a one-hole punch. Into her pencil cup go ballpoint pens, sharpened pencils, and a dagger-shaped letter opener some former reference librarian must have left behind. I think of her sitting here, opening this drawer, seeing it clean and fully stocked. I open and close the drawer several times, just looking. Yvonne will say, *Margo worked very hard on that desk for you, Patricia*, and Patricia will smile and thank me, and despite my Donna-shaped reservations, we'll begin to be friends.

No. We will not be friends. "Friends" turned out very badly last time. It didn't start that way, of course—it started beautifully. Meeting in line at the hospital cafeteria, reaching for the same slice of lackluster quiche. "Lackluster quiche," Donna quipped at our shared table. "That's what the sign should say!" Dissolving in fits of laughter over this, feeling layers of wariness, years of loneliness, melt away. And then hours spent chatting over steaming cups in the bland chain café across from the hospital. It didn't matter where we were! We were building our vigorous bond. We used to parade ourselves everywhere as a pair: Jane and Donna, Donna and Jane. More like sisters than workmates. Until I started to open my mouth and let certain things out. Certain phrases, ideas, like, *The ones that die are the lucky ones*. That's when the sliver of ice came between us. Donna's icy green eyes. Her lame excuses for canceling plans. How she stared, in that room the last time. Her obvious disgust much louder than if she'd shouted out.

So Patricia will not be a friend. I'll be *friendly*, like I am with Liz and Nasrin. But why should I even be friendly with someone who reminds me of Donna? I'll do my best to steer clear, to smile from a distance. Be polite but closed off.

Not Margo's forte—and it wasn't Jane's, either.

"You're all decked out," Liz says, striding over from the circ desk. She has no idea she's seeing me as I used to be, during surgery, at least—wearing gloves and a mask. She watches me spray the desk's surface and wipe it clean. "The cleaners can do that, you know," she says, but I ignore her and focus on the desktop's shine. Eventually, she drifts away. When I've finished and peeled the gloves from my sweaty hands, I feel twin things: the deep satisfaction that comes from a job well done, and the sense of loss that always follows on its heels. *I had a project. Now I don't*, I think, trying hard not to drift toward nostalgia for the old days. It helps that Yvonne thinks I've performed some kind of miracle. "Margo, you've outdone yourself," she says, looking wide-eyed at the newly arranged and spotless station. Nasrin and Liz admire it, too, Liz grudgingly, I'm sure. They open and close the drawers to murmur over how neatly I've organized them. But once they've left, the emptiness yawns wide once more. *I had a project. Now I don't.* In the bathroom mirror downstairs, I look at my sweaty, pallid face. I don't feel clean; I need a bath. I feel it like an itch all over my skin. Like a layer of filth. When I get home, I'll sink into my tub and that will do it. I'll get a reset. Emptiness and unease banished.

◆ ◆ ◆

The bath doesn't do it. While I'm still pink-skinned, I throw a light coat on over my pajamas, slide into flip-flops, and leave my apartment door ajar. It's eight p.m. but already dark—the parking lot is full. Most people are home from work, eating dinner, watching TV. They aren't looking out their windows. I make my way past the cars to the small patch of woods beyond them, carrying my lighter and a memento from my past: a worn blue scrubs top. I've balled it up and stuffed it into my coat pocket. I find a well-hidden spot about halfway through the trees and gather branches quickly; this will be a small fire, a brief fire. After clearing all the brush from a wide circle of dirt, I pile the sticks carefully, get the blaze going, pull out the shirt, and throw it on the flames. There's a soft *whoosh*. I watch the fire eat away at the fabric, eat it all the way to black, and then to nothingness, ash. The flames give off an antiseptic smell, a hospital smell—or have I imagined it? When it's gone, there's a new lightness in my belly. I sweep away the ash and bits of charred wood with my foot, then I walk back home feeling free.

Sometimes, when the bath fails, the fire succeeds.

Fire succeeds: that's something I learned as a child—standing safely back from a house ablaze—and I've never forgotten it.

◆　◆　◆

The remaining weekdays pass. I float through them in my usual way: chatting with patrons and coworkers, moving without pause through my duties on the main floor. Nothing disturbs the flow of days, but *I* am disturbed. In my head I name it: *Pa-tree-see-ah is coming*. I stare at the empty reference desk, imagine how she'll be sitting there across from me, training her Donna-like gaze on my every move. So foolish, I know. She'll just be *working* there, minding her business. And I'll be minding mine. Even so, I can't bathe or burn the anxiety out of me. Behind my cool Margo façade, I'm trembling. Invisibly, I hope.

By Friday, I'm in a state. I watch Friday Guy arrive, settle in, place his bags around his feet, and scoot the chair close to the monitor. His eyes dart to mine, telling me he's dipping in, pulling up illicit sites. My gut pulls me to him, but my feet won't move. Liz and Nasrin are breathing down my neck; they want their Friday treat, too. "He's doing it, Margo. He's looking at those sites. He's not even hiding it," Liz whispers urgently. But however much they push me—and however much I want to be pushed—I can't obey the urge.

"I think I'll let him be today," I say. I'm glad to hear how calm, how controlled, I sound, even as they murmur their disbelief. I stare hard at Friday Guy until he glances up, gives me that look of his—a punished schoolboy's, but lustful, yearning, too. I have to turn away from him and busy myself with the hold books to resist his pull. The minutes tick by. Finally, I hear him stand to collect his bags: that rustle of plastic. When he passes the circ desk, I panic and almost call out to stop him. But how strange would that be? How desperate, how un-Margo-like?

When I'm certain he's gone, I pick up the cleaning spray and paper towels we keep behind the desk and march over to his station. I clean everything: keyboard, mouse, monitor, screen, desk, and chair—almost as thorough a cleaning as I gave Patricia's desk days ago. For ten minutes or so, I'm swept back into that focused, purposeful place. When I'm done, I stand there, panting a little, staring at the purified station. It's like I've erased him. A wave of absolute longing slips through my body like water.

He'll be back next Friday, of course, brimming with lust for that virtual flesh—and for my interference—so there's no use being dramatic. It's nothing but a pause in our long and titillating back-and-forth. But I can't say that out loud to Liz and Nasrin. "Well, that's tidied," I say instead, breezing back to stow the supplies. Liz purses her lips but doesn't say a word, still stewing over the loss of our Friday diversion. She sits frowning at her screen. *Spring Books—Sneak Peek!* reads the headline on the website page she's scanning. She's as regular with her book lists as Friday Guy is with his porn.

And so the week ends.

The weekend is scattered, windy. I catch myself watching trash blow by in the grocery store parking lot. It fills me with terror. Is that all I am? But I'm not, I'm not. I look at my feet in my shoes, standing firm on the Carlyle ground. *I'm not going anywhere.*

◆ ◆ ◆

Monday morning, 9:10 a.m. I waited as long as I could. "I'm Margo," I say, offering Patricia my hand. She arrived early, and she's been seated at the reference desk, looking through her immaculate, organized drawer. Now she pops up to shake my hand.

"Pa-tree-thee-ah," she says, with a slight lisp I didn't hear when we first met. "I know. The new reference librarian.

Welcome," I say, smiling. "I cleaned your desk. This whole area was basically storage. No one's sat here for—" "Twelve years, yes." She nods, looking around. "I've heard." Even that reminds me of Donna—the abrupt way she finished my sentence just now. I search her face for some kind of physical resemblance: the shape of her nose, the slant of her cheekbones. But there's nothing. She's no near or distant relative of Donna's; she doesn't know Donna, and she doesn't know *me*. She thanks me then and I tell her it was no trouble, that I was glad to do it, and then we nod together, subsiding into silence. My heart is beating frantically and I'm afraid of blurting something silly out when Yvonne calls, "Patricia!" and steps between us. Yvonne tells her she hopes she's settling in okay, and then I'm dismissed. I tell Patricia it was nice meeting her, though I want to say: *It was weird meeting you. It was disturbing meeting you.* Patricia gives me a distracted smile.

Back at my perch, I watch Patricia listen as Yvonne walks her through the policies handbook. Patricia nods along as if she understands completely, has heard it all before. It's her first day, but she radiates confidence. My own first day was a blur; I felt fevered and foolish and made too many jokes. I was too bright, too loud, too *everything*. Patricia, though— Patricia is perfect.

Until she isn't.

She makes her way to us at the circ desk around two p.m., looking out of sorts. I saw her answering a call or two over there; maybe she got a squirrelly one. It happens. But she tells us she's had calls that "don't seem like reference calls"—she leans hard on the word *reference* to make sure Nasrin and I get it. We do—and we're holding back laughs. I know just what she means: the spell-a-random-word-for-me calls, the what's-the-nearest-adult-novelty-store calls, the tell-me-what-the-weather-is-in-London-today calls. "We used to take all those calls ourselves," I tell her. "But now that you're here, Yvonne said we should start forwarding them to you." She blinks for a moment, eyes huge behind her lenses. Disbelieving. "I see," she says finally, though I'm certain she doesn't. I think there's a chance she'll pack up and leave Carlyle tonight, and shouldn't that make me happy? It should. "You'll get better calls soon," I blurt, though it's a lie. I don't know why I've said it. Nasrin agrees, and I see Patricia relax. I relax, too.

While I'm checking out a pile of comic books for two teens, I glance Patricia's way: stylish and sleek, she's like a rare bird over there, flaunting her feathers in the gloom. She radiates coolness, too. I look around, trying to see the library through her eyes: the water stains on the ceiling; the faded gray love seat in YA; the drawn faces of our computer users, washed deadly white or gray in the light of their screens. Will she stay in a place like this? Or just land here for a while, before flitting away?

I turn my full attention back to the teens. These ones aren't so bad; they're nervous and shy, with acne-pitted skin and mouths full of metal. "You kids have any schoolwork to do, or are these comic books your homework?" I ask, and they titter. "They're manga," the boy says, but not unkindly, not haughtily. I know what manga are—after two years, I've learned—but I play along anyway. While we're chatting, I sense Patricia's eyes on me, her interest warming my skin. *What brought you here, Margo?* she's wondering. But when I look up, she's picking through the desk drawers. Examining a ruler. Not the least bit interested in learning my story, of course. Who am I, to her? My spirits sag a little as I say good-bye to the teens.

Just behind them is Julia Mather, one of our top five local eccentrics. It's like she popped up out of nowhere with her long, flyaway gray hair, her gnarled hands and glossy red nails. It's hard not to stare at those nails as she gestures wildly; she's clearly worked up. "I've returned several books in that metal box outside and you all continue to lose them." I wait for a beat. She'll go on. Julia always goes on. "I returned one just the other day and now it's listed as lost and apparently I owe money. My taxes pay your salaries here, you know!" We do know. Julia has told us many times; other patrons have, too. "If the book is lost—" I start. "But it isn't. I returned it to the metal box," Julia insists. My fingers tap quickly across the keyboard to bring up her record. "Ah," I say. With one hand, with one set of red nails, she twitches a long strand of hair over her shoulder. I stare at the screen, pretending to be lost in thought. Usually Julia amuses me; today, though, she simply annoys me. I try to breathe and relax my face. I had patients like her, of course—domineering ones who were always right, no matter what the nurses and doctors said or did. But patients were easier to deal with: half-naked and vulnerable in their hospital gowns, shivering with illness or fear even as they struggled for power. You knew they wanted comfort, reassurance, more than anything, and it was easy to provide. I never raised my voice once, like some others did; I only smiled and soothed them—with words or a quick jab. A shame I can't do that with Julia.

I stare at her coldly, scanning her body. When she was younger, she must have been beautifully slim. Now she's the kind of thin that makes your skin hurt to look at her. Her nails are hidden under glossy color, but I bet they're ridged and bumpy—signs of ill health. And her dry, rasping cough doesn't bode well, either, but who knows? People like her can live off bitterness for years. Unless someone helps them. Nudges them over the rim.

"What is it? What does it say?" Julia leans forward, breaking the spell as she cranes her neck toward my screen. I refuse to turn it toward her, though I'm supposed to. "I see one book here that is long overdue. *The Rise of Towson Manor*, by J. S. Cullen?" She nods vigorously. "That's the one. Go out there and check. Go out there right now and you'll see. It's there." In my mind, I'm lifting her up in the air, rattling her bones. Dropping her back down. "That isn't my job, Mrs. Mather. Other staff members do that regularly. If it were in the box, they would have found it by now, and we'd see it here in the system." I tap my screen. Julia rears up, lifting her hands with her voice. "This is the forty-fourth book of mine you've lost. I won't pay this library a cent! I pay your salary, you know, and everyone's salary here!" She rakes her nails through the air to include us all: the layabouts who profit from Julia's bounteous wealth.

Patricia is watching. *Everyone* is watching.

I have the urge to bark out an angry laugh, but I beat it

back. "I'm afraid this is the forty-fourth book of *ours* that *you've* lost, Mrs. Mather," I say quietly, leaning close and staring into her rheumy blue eyes. Just as her quivering lips open to protest, I lean even closer. "Now go home and find that book. Go home and find the other books, too. If you don't, you'll be paying a hefty fine, one that's long overdue. I'll collect it myself." It's the voice I would have used on Friday Guy, if I'd indulged myself last week. Julia takes two stumbling steps back. I think she'll make a fuss but then her hands wilt at her sides. She steps farther back from the desk, staring at me. Then she turns suddenly and shuttles through the door, her curtain of gray hair flying behind her.

So, I win—of course I do. Jane always won, too, but those wins were more definitive, and they exist in a world unreachable from here. For an instant, I get a wave of hospital smell, like I did when I burned my scrubs the other night. I look around, but there's no evident source. A patron? They sometimes bounce between hospitals and here, bringing the scents of each place with them. I scan the main floor but there's nothing to see, and it's not like I can go around sniffing everyone.

"What was that?" Yvonne emerges from the office, dimples nonexistent, a quizzical look on her face. She doesn't like a fuss. But looking around, it's hard to say there ever was one. The whole room is tranquil as a lake. Patrons sitting quietly in patches of sun, undisturbed, like turtles sunning themselves on rocks. Others drifting slowly through the aisles.

But there *was* a fuss, of course, and my nerves are still

singing with it: my cheeks are hot and my underarms are damp. *Calm down*, I tell myself. *Calm down, for god's sake.*

"It was nothing," I tell Yvonne. "Just Julia Mather being—herself." This wins me a dimpled smile and a satisfied nod from Yvonne. No one needs to say much more than "Julia Mather" for the rest of us to understand. We go through this once a month or so: Julia comes in, airing her eternal complaint, and we respond in our brusque, eternal ways. It's a dance we do. Usually, I pace calmly through the moves, even with Julia nearly spitting in my face. The difference, today, was how close I came to swerving off the path.

I go on checking out books, offering patrons my smiles and chitchat. "The weather is changing so fast. I was cold walking here this morning!" "You love this author, don't you? How many books of his have you read?" "Did you see our Hispanic Heritage Month display? You might find something there." All the while, I'm seeing Julia's shocked face, her hair flying behind her as she marched out the door. Then I imagine her tucked under sheets, her eyes begging for help. Those red nails clutching fabric. The fabric of the sheets, then the fabric of my shirt—the one I burned. *Help me*, she mouths. I have to stifle a moan.

This vision leads me to Ms. Jensen: my very last patient. I was meticulous in my care of her. Brushed her long gray hair—like Julia's, but better maintained—with the hairbrush her husband had left on the bedside table. Fed her ice chips with a spoon. Spooned the medicine into her mouth, too, a little at a time, with encouraging words. *Come on. There you go. Good girl.* Held her hand as she seized. And seized again, staring, wild-eyed. I got down close to her face and gazed into those eyes, so vast, the pupils wide and black—and then shrinking, shrinking. This was the private ritual I'd been carrying out for years, but that time a familiar voice startled me: *What the fuck are you doing, Jane?* It was Donna. My dear old friend Donna. I'd never been caught before; all I could do was gape at her as she pressed the call button and summoned them all. It had been so peaceful just moments before—only Ms. Jensen gasping, only the two of us with our eyes locked together—and then Donna and the rest came crowding into the room with their terrible noise. Dr. Abdul slapping on rubber gloves, the nurses handling Ms. Jensen like a dead fish. All of them shoving me aside. As I backed out of the room, no one noticed but Donna. Why she didn't scream I'll never know. Some last vestige of loyalty? Or maybe I'd shocked the sound right out of her. I stopped in the break room, stuffed my belongings from my locker into a plastic bag, and walked quickly, my shoes squeaking all the way to the sliding glass doors.

I looked back once, though I shouldn't have. No one was there. Just the hallway, shining like water. It already felt alien and remote, like every other place from my past: cramped old family home, threadbare apartment, sickly yellow-tiled grade school. Sadness welled up in me so fast that I had to vomit in the parking lot. Then I stood and walked straight-backed to my exhausted little car.

I drove—burying Jane and building Margo, mile after mile.

Patricia looks up. I realize I've been staring, so I smile,

raise my hand in an awkward wave. She smiles, too, but then looks away. I watch her study her screen and then scribble down notes in her notebook. Studious. Alone. She's so shiny and new that no one knows what to do with her. Patrons avoid her. Liz and Nasrin have whispered about her, but they stiffen when she comes near. It's her first day, so I expect this to change. As she writes, brow furrowed, I'm convinced for a moment that she's transcribing my memory: the deathbed scene, the awful commotion, Donna's clenched face, and my chucking up sickness in the parking lot before speeding away for good.

But she can't be, of course. She couldn't have seen any of that. She's just a woman at a new job, taking notes.

Even so, I can't fully relax until I'm home and sliding into steaming hot water. My god, it's good to scald yourself nearly to death. All the day's strangeness evaporates. I lie there, utterly calm and free, looking down the length of my bodily landscape. The tips of my breasts rise like islands out of the water, as they always do, as they've always done, except when I was little, and the water would swallow me, and I'd look down and see nothing, as if I'd vanished. That was a great comfort to me then. I slide all the way under now, like I did back then, though the tub is more cramped than it used to be. Now I have to contort myself to get all the way under, but I manage it, and hold my breath for as long as I can, then come up out of it with a great, cleansing exhale.

After a while, a chill grips me. I've lain here too long. The dead memories inch back: the sheen of Ms. Jensen's hair when I brushed it that last day, the sun just starting to lighten the sky when I left the hospital forever. I open my eyes abruptly, grip the sides of the tub, and push myself up. That was the past. *The past.* I blame Patricia's arrival for bringing it all up. That tilt to her head, that knowing glint in her brown eyes. I reach for my robe, tie it around me tightly. Enough nonsense.

I make myself hot milk with honey to chase away the chill, just like my mother did when I couldn't sleep. She was gentle with me in the middle of the night, though her whiskey breath was all I could smell as I gulped my drink. I woke in the night more often than I should have to share those moments with her, just the two of us, when she was boozy and loose and I was drowsy with warm milk. Then she'd abruptly say, *Go on. Go back to bed.*

◆ ◆ ◆

By Friday, I've gotten used to the sight of Patricia, across from me at her post, reminding me of Donna. She hardly moves. Her hand and arm slide across and down the page, her eyes flick back and forth from screen to page, page to screen, but that's it. She isn't roaming, isn't exploring the stacks or even her own reference collection, as far as I can tell. She's young, though, and I suppose everything worth anything is computerized, to her. Yvonne seems content to let her feel her way into the job; she must be happy just to have someone sitting there, attractively filling the seat at the reference desk.

Meanwhile, the rest of us keep things humming. I hardly rest my behind in the chair before I'm hopping up again to grab a book on hold for someone, or to help someone print in color from her phone. I wonder if Patricia's aware of this at all—how still and static she is in the midst of our flow. She seems mostly oblivious, but sometimes I feel her watching me. Whenever I glance up, she's looked away, but I know that prickly sensation. I felt it back then, in the old life, when Donna would watch me injecting saline into a patient's IV. Saline! She hovered like that, toward the end, pretending to chat as I did my rounds. But her eyes were on me all the while, or they'd flit to the syringe, checking it, checking me, nonchalantly pressing the patient's wrist for his pulse. As if I would have done something then—as if, after all our months of friendship, she thought I'd be so careless!

As the hours creep by, I feel done with all this nonsense of Patricia. Ready for more steadfast diversions. I look at the clock: 2:36. Friday Guy should have been here by now. There's a tremor in my knees as I walk the floor, willing him to come.

I'm so out of sorts by three o'clock—*thirty minutes* past his usual time—that when Yvonne comes to the circ desk, I blurt, "How's she getting on?" tilting my head toward Patricia. I hope Patricia herself didn't hear, though my voice was louder than I intended. "Fine," Yvonne says, nodding and smiling, looking vaguely satisfied. "Does she—what does she *do*?" Yvonne chuckles. "She's still getting the lay of the land. But she'll be weeding our reference materials, and expanding our electronic resources, too. And answering reference calls, of course." Yvonne and I stand there in silence, watching Patricia. She looks like a diligent schoolgirl, one of those overachievers. Is that what's needed in the library? I shrug. Her library must be different from mine: more scholarly and removed, above it all. Maybe that's the realm of the reference desk. "Okay," I say, because I can't say anything else.

The minutes tick longer into Friday Guy's absence. I watch the front door while replaying last Friday's neglect. How he looked at me, practically begging me to interfere. How he walked out, forlorn. How I wiped down his station, cleaning all trace of him away. I'm on the verge of tears when Liz sidles up. "Looks like you took care of our porno fanatic," she says. I glare at her but she doesn't stop. "I wonder where he'll end up—Breese Public Library? Germantown? They're stricter there, though. The director—" "Enough!" I roar, regretting it at once. The way Liz's face falls, then hardens, and Nasrin rears back. The way patrons snap their heads up. Patricia, too.

I shake my head and force out a chuckle.

"Forgive me, Liz, I'm so keyed up today!" I say a little too loud but better, softer than a moment ago. I ad-lib a story: how I've been caring for a sick aunt in Pinckneyville, spending late nights there, no hope of her recovery. When Liz and Nasrin are nearly in tears, murmuring in sympathy, I tell them all about the family scuffle for Auntie Lou's money, how disgraceful it is, how I only want her antique dining set for sentimental reasons, and by the end, my coworkers are furious at my fantasy relatives. My small outburst has been utterly forgotten. The patrons have long since looked away, and Patricia is back to staring at her screen.

What a week. What a strange, unforeseeable, nerve-rattling week. I'm glad it's coming to an end.

But when I walk out at five, the sudden freedom of the

weekend descends like a crushing weight. I haven't felt this way since my first weeks here, when the end of each day made me tremble and sweat. Now I look up at the already darkening sky, at the red and yellow leaves on the trees, and I tremble. I sweat.

I feel chased all the way home, like there's someone right on my heels. I take the blue metal stairs two at a time, slam and lock the apartment door behind me, and run hot water into the bath. I'm still looking over my shoulder, like a fool, as I strip off my clothes. It's not until I lower myself into the tub, gingerly at first, and then all at once, sending a wave up the side of the tub and a little over, that I feel some relief. Some, but not enough.

♦ ♦ ♦

Come Monday, I stride through the front door with an urgency I can barely contain. I practically jogged here this morning, I was walking so fast. Wet leaves under my feet as the grass begins to brown. The weekend was a respite, yes. Didn't want it to last a minute longer, though, and gratefully awoke to the sound of my alarm. I glance toward Reference and see Patricia already there. She looks up. Smiles distractedly. She's beginning to remind me of Donna less—or that's what I tell myself.

At the circ desk, Nasrin sets up for the day. I say my hellos, my how-are-yous, how-was-your-weekends, then collect a cart full of returns from the metal box Julia Mather so despises. After checking the books back in, I begin my reshelving rounds. New releases first, then mysteries, romance, and science fiction. Mystery returns far outnumber the others, as usual. I hum a little tune under my breath, sliding one book after another into its spot. I used to hum like this as a nurse, too. *Stop that damned noise*, one red-faced man growled at me from his bed while I prepared his medications. He was a doll, though, really—a poor broken doll I held in the dead of night as he swiped at tears. He longed for his deceased wife and their former house, long since sold to a young family. He'd be going home to his "lousy, empty apartment," he told me with a bitter grin.

Not long after, he died of what the doctor said was a stroke. He'd been recovering from minor surgery but you just never knew, did you, one of my nurse friends said, shaking her head.

Nasrin finds me in the stacks a few minutes later. She's wild-eyed and nearly in tears. "Margo, come quick. To the ladies' bathroom. Please." I ask her what's happened as we hustle down the stairs, but she can't seem to say more; only, "Hurry," even though we *are* hurrying. We stop at the door to the restroom and she steps aside. "I can't," she says as tears spill down her cheeks. Sweet Nasrin. It's probably a toilet full of turds or a watery mess on the floor. It's happened before, and I've been the one to survey the scene and alert the cleaning staff. Sometimes I've even cleaned it up myself, if it isn't too bad. I've seen and done worse. Much worse. My coworkers here are soft as snails.

I push open the door and let it swing shut behind me. My god, the smell. I clamp my hand over my mouth and nose and try to call up my once-ingrained immunity to stench. I can't do it, though; it's gone. Even so, I peel my hand from my face and force myself to breathe: inhaling deeply, then forcing the air out. It steadies me. I peer past the sinks on the right and see a huddled mass on the floor of the last stall. Legs jutting out along the mint-colored tiles, bony feet in shiny black flats. Familiar-looking, those feet in those shoes. I can't place them yet, though. I take another deep breath—letting the foul air fill my chest, lungs, and stomach—and then I expel it. Loudly. I walk quickly to the handicapped stall, push at the door. It swings wide, bangs against the wall, and below me I see the staring eyes and the gaping, still-quivering wet mouth of Julia Mather.

She's wedged in by the toilet. I crawl closer and peer into her face. It's slack, but her eyes are wide. Eyelids fluttering. I can hear her take a shallow breath and then pause. Another shallow breath, then a longer pause. I put my face close to hers, smell the fetid breath pouring from her mouth, and feel electricity pulse along my nerves. She's close, so close to the end. I pull her down, away from the toilet, so I can comfortably straddle her with my chest pressed to hers, my face hovering less than an inch from hers. Her pupils are widening, the dark inching outward from the center bit by bit, consuming the blue.

At the sight of it, I moan.

There's knocking at the bathroom door. Someone pushes it open a crack. I scramble to my feet.

"Margo? What's going on in there? Is everything all right? Is it—is she *dead*?" It's Liz. She whispers the last word. "Everything's fine. Just close the door. Leave it closed. I'll deal with it." I sound convincing, I think, if out of breath. "We called 911," Liz tells me. I grit my teeth. "Fine. Close the door."

The door bangs shut, and I'm alone. Alone again with Julia. Lovely, fading Julia. I lie back down along the length of her. Her eyes have widened more, her mouth has stilled. I feel it in my own chest when she draws a shallow breath. I try to breathe with her, to hold my own breath until my chest burns. But when I breathe, it's deep and forceful. It flutters the wisps of gray hair framing her face. It doesn't disturb her eyes, though, which are almost fully black. No longer blue like mine. The prickling sensation runs through me again, warming my core. My heartbeat quickens and my breath comes fast. The wisps of her hair pulse in time with it. My eyes stay glued to the black, to—

The door squeals open. The sound of low heels marching in.

"I told you, Liz, just leave this to me!" It explodes out of me. The footsteps pause for a moment, then continue on. I try to scramble up from the floor, but I've wedged myself so tightly against Julia this time that I fumble and fall against her.

Whoever it is has walked to the stall.

"Margo?" Patricia says. As if she isn't sure what she's looking at, as if the tangled heap I am with Julia might have a different name, a new name, other than the one she learned a week ago. "Yes?" I say, but it's muffled against Julia's shirt, where my face has landed. I work to push myself up and manage to rise to a seated position. I lean against the wall. I see myself through Patricia's eyes: red-faced and sweaty, disheveled. The tail of my shirt has pulled out of my pants, and my hair has come loose from its habitual bun. My reading glasses hang limply around my neck; I forgot they were there. I try to give her a confident, challenging look. "What is it?" I ask. As if she's a patron who's come up to the circ desk with a trivial question when I'm in the middle of something important. Patricia says nothing, simply reaches out a hand. I stare at it. I'm reluctant to pull away from Julia, from what *was* Julia. I look down at her—one last look at the staring eyes, the slack mouth, all of her finally still—before taking Patricia's hand and letting her help me up.

"I missed it," I say aloud, without meaning to. And then I burst into tears. Patricia says nothing at first, but then she pulls me to her and pats my back as I cry. "I know, I know," she whispers. It startles me. *What does she know? What could she possibly know?* Even so, I sink into her, let her hold me, comfort me. She must think I'm mourning Julia, our longtime, troublesome patron. She must think I'm weeping because I tried to save her and failed.

"I know," Patricia says again, firmly, authoritatively. Maybe she *does* know, I think; maybe she knows everything somehow. And understands—forgives me, even, for everything I've done. Maybe I was right to think she read my mind when I relived Ms. Jensen's death the other day. I lift my head up and stare into her solemn brown eyes. I don't know how I could have mistaken her for Donna. Patricia would never do what Donna did. Patricia *saw* me; she held me close, and then she pulled me up to stand.

I let her lead me from the bathroom.

It's a beautiful thing, to be seen and understood. To be cared for.

After years of caring for others, I hardly know how to receive such care. When we exit the bathroom and see Nasrin there, and Liz with her arms folded over her chest, looking peeved, I turn to Patricia.

"The woman is dead," she says. Nasrin wails and covers her face with her hands.

PATRICIA

I wouldn't be here if I'd sold my novel. That's the dismal thought that comes to me as I push open the Carlyle Public Library's front door and instantly smell mildew. I start to breathe through my mouth, but I won't be able to do that all day, five days a week, if I take the job here.

If, ha. If I'm offered the job, I'll have to take it. I just hope my clothes won't start to reek of mildew, and then my skin and hair . . . *Stop.* I touch my hair anyway, as if it were already tainted.

At least the building doesn't look moldy. It's beautiful, in fact. I have a thing for old library buildings. This one was built in 1890, back when libraries were the new palaces for the people, and looked it. I imagine it back then: a solid, imposing, brick mass beside the dirt roads and shabby storefronts of late-nineteenth-century Main Street. People would have strolled by to gawk at it, this fine building filled with books. I stare around at the high, arched ceilings and dark wood paneling, all of it original, I would guess. This isn't a *bad* place. A little musty, yes, but light filled and warm. Welcoming, too. When my eyes finish roaming, they land on the person staring at me from behind the circulation desk: a tall and broad-shouldered woman in a baby-blue dress. Fitted at the waist, with unseasonal short sleeves. Her dark hair is pulled into a tidy bun. She could have stepped right out of the 1800s herself, one of those ancient librarians I learned about in my History of Libraries course.

When I approach the desk and ask for Yvonne Matthews, she fixes me with her sharp blue eyes. I give her my name and see her eyebrows lift at the pronunciation. I could have just said "Pa-trish-a," the way I sometimes do, but what if I end up working here? I want them to know how to pronounce it. "Delmarco," I add, feeling heat rise to my cheeks. "Patricia Delmarco."

The woman turns to get Yvonne, a short Black woman with close-cropped hair and a generous smile. Back in her office, Yvonne and I exchange niceties, and then she spends most of the time telling me her plans for improving the library, beginning with hiring someone for the reference desk. "We haven't had the funds for over twelve years," she says, looking pained. "But now we do. The board is behind it. And we want someone like you who's fresh out of school and has exciting ideas for bringing us into the twenty-first century."

Fresh out of school. I stare at the colorful, bad landscape paintings adorning the walls behind Yvonne's desk and feel intensely nostalgic for library school: for my cushy part-time job in the grad school library; my mostly tedious courses; the smart, quirky company of up-and-coming librarians; and the cozy *idea* of being practical. The *concept* of playing it safe, of securing a safety net while still devoting most of my time to finishing, perfecting, and selling my novel. *When I sell my novel*, I'd think to myself. *When I sell my novel*. Never "if," always "when." It was never a dream—it was fact. It was real to me. Much more real than the thought of sitting where I am now, interviewing for a job at a small public library, with the old life—the old me—discarded like trash.

Yet here I sit. Dan thinks I should hold out for something better—and by "better" he means: something, anything, in Chicago. "An urban library would be much more in line with your training and interests," he's said, like a guidance counselor, but what he really meant was: *Don't leave me. Please don't leave me.* He wants to keep me locked in our sweet Chicago life, but the sweetness has faded for me lately: in the clutch of his neediness, and in the wake of my dead dream of writing. I've found it hard to breathe, some nights, with his heavy leg thrown over mine in our once-cozy double bed. I haven't said this to Dan; I've simply told him I need to jump-start my career, and that Carlyle is the only remotely livable in-state place hiring a reference librarian right now. *And it isn't far*, I've reminded him. *We'll be able to visit.* He's given me a seasick look when I've said that.

"Are you interested?" Yvonne asks me now. "Excuse me?" I say, though I did hear her question. I know how I have to respond, but I can't help delaying. She chuckles. "Would you like the job? It's yours, if you want it. You're our best candidate by far, and I think you'd fit in nicely here." I keep my face straight at the thought of my "fitting in nicely" and manage to smile. *It's a job,* I remind myself. *I need a job.* "Of course," I say after a moment. "I'd be delighted to work here. I'm thrilled." I stretch my mouth to its limits and extend my hand. "When can I start?"

That's it. An animated Yvonne begins telling me details, finding paperwork for me to fill out and sign. I hear a door slam shut, and lock, in my mind. Though it's actually a drawer. My desk drawer, the one where I buried my book. I did it days ago, with hot tears running down my cheeks as I swiped at my nose—like a child. An angry, entitled, tantruming child. *Bam. Click.* The same sounds now, but distant, echoing. Like something someone else did, ages ago.

◆　◆　◆

The following days are a flurry of apartment-searching, packing, and pacing through emotional upheaval with Dan. I don't feel anything much—because I'm numb, because I'm on my way out the door to something new, if not desirable— but he's a wreck. I can tell from his red-rimmed eyes, and his silence during our last shared meals. "I'll see you in a month," I tell him, with an edge to my voice. His sadness makes me impatient, unkind. He nods his head heavily and musters a smile. When he regains his composure just before I leave, I know what he's thinking: *This can't be real. This move is just a passing phase, a lark.* It's possible he's right.

◆ ◆ ◆

I show up for my first day of work in Chicago style: I'm in nearly all black except for a pop of red, the red of my silk shell. I feel overdressed, a little ridiculous, especially when I reach my antiquated desk. I sit there, thumbing through the contents of my drawers, not really sure what to do with myself. How do I make myself into a reference librarian—in the real world, outside of school? Do I even remember how to conduct a reference interview, how to get to the core of the problem a patron is trying to solve? *Make eye contact.* That's all I can remember right now. And: *Do not interrupt.* That's it. I'm slightly panicking and starting to Google "how to conduct reference interview" when I look up to see the large woman from the circ desk hustling over, wearing another awful dress and sensible low-heeled shoes. For a moment I think she'll career right into my desk—she moves with such force.

She doesn't. She stops neatly, a few inches away. I push my red-framed glasses up my nose.

"I'm Margo," she says, offering me her hand. I take it and enjoy that rare thing: a firm and satisfying handshake. Even Yvonne, who seems so vigorous, put a wilting fish in my hands when we met.

"Patricia," I tell her. I see her focus on my lips, and then she moves her mouth as if she's saying my name to herself, tasting something new. Something different from the usual Midwestern meat-and-potatoes fare: *Joyce, Barb, Sandy, Mel.* But *Margo* doesn't fit with those, either; it has a touch of flair. It matches the regal way she carries herself, though she looks thoroughly of Carlyle, too, with her solid build and milky pale skin. When her blue eyes glint above the great, beaming warmth of her smile, I suddenly have to swallow back a laugh—and I can't say why. It feels like we're sharing a joke, though we've only just met.

"I know. The new reference librarian. Welcome," she says. She tells me that she cleaned and organized my desk, and I thank her. I'm not sure what else to say—she seems to need something more from me that I'm not equipped to give. Soon the light in her eyes fades above her smiling mouth, leaving me feeling strained and remote; I don't make more of an effort to speak because I can't really touch this life, or believe in it, even as I'm beginning to live it. Moments later, Yvonne swoops in. I feel an odd twinge as I watch Margo's retreating back; I want her to stay. We have plenty of shared days ahead of us, though—a thought that sends dread rolling through me. Not because of Margo herself, but because here I am, committing myself to this job that signals the end of my writerly life. Such as it was. If Dan were here, he'd tell me not to "universalize." "Start something new," he suggested once, with the lighthearted ignorance of the noncreative. "I bet you'll feel better." Right. With that four-hundred-page albatross of an unpublished novel weighing me down? Why— and how—should I start something new with that deadweight telling me I can't write, can't publish, can't progress? But there was no use asking him any of that.

Dan has his merits, but I can't recall them right now, as I listen to Yvonne with one ear, watch her flipping through the neatly tabbed employee handbook. I nod and murmur when

I feel it's needed. Dan isn't here, hasn't said a word, of course, but I hear him anyway, and stew on his remembered words: *Don't universalize. Start something new.* Well, I'm starting something new now, aren't I?

At ten o'clock, my desk phone rings for the first time; I'm unprepared. I've been staring at the screen, examining the library website. It's so backward, the resources so minimal and outdated that it's making my head hurt. This will be a colossal job. "Reference desk, um, how can I help you?" I manage. "Good morning. Can you tell me what time *Amanda's Grace* is on tonight?" the caller asks. I think I've misheard her. I ask her to repeat herself and she does, practically shouting it this time, as if my hearing were the problem. "I'm sorry, I can hear you perfectly fine but I . . . don't understand the question," I say, hoping my voice won't carry to the circ desk. Now the woman talks to me as if I'm slow, rather than deaf. "It's a television show. It's on tonight, but I don't know when." "So you're calling the library?" "Yes, ma'am." She's undaunted by how incredulous I sound. "I don't have a computer here at home. Got a TV, though!" she chuckles. An elderly woman, alone at home, looking forward to her TV show. However strange it is that she should call, I humor her and look it up online. "Eight o'clock on CBS," I tell her. "Enjoy your show." She thanks me, calls me sweetheart, and hangs up. I sit staring at the phone. What the hell was that? I want to tell someone about it, and I look over at Margo, thinking she'd appreciate it. She's laughing with another circulation clerk, a young Middle Eastern woman I haven't met yet. Margo's head is thrown back; she's holding her hands over her heart as if shocked with delight. I can't help but smile, watching her, thinking that, somehow, she knows—that I've told her about my call, and that's why she's laughing. It makes me feel less alone.

"How far is it from Coopersville to Marsten?" another caller, my second one, asks with no preamble. One offbeat call was funny—charming, even—but two? I fight back my irritation, use Google Maps, and tell him: twenty-three miles. There's a third call, too. I hang on to hope until the man asks: "Can you tell me the number for Walmart customer service?" When we're finished, I slam down the phone. Is this a joke? Why am I getting these calls? I remember my Reference Services class, all the time we spent learning the kinds of questions we'd encounter in the wild. Things like "What resources would you recommend for researching X?" or "Where can I find information on Y?" Nothing like "How far to a nearby town?" A fact easily looked up on a laptop or phone. I'm certain there's been a mistake. I push my glasses up my nose and walk over to the circ desk. Margo and the other woman— Nasrin, she tells me—look up and smile. Nasrin is gorgeous, her green eyes bright against the dark fabric of her hijab. She radiates kindness. Softness. Next to her, Margo stands like a blue-and-white tower. "Um, I've had a few calls transferred to me so far that don't seem like *reference* calls." Both women blink at me, then Margo shrugs. "We used to take all those calls ourselves. But now that you're here, Yvonne said we should start forwarding them to you." "I see," I say, but I don't. Not at all. I see that the calls fall under the broad category of "information," and that "reference" includes information, but . . . is this what I paid fifteen grand a year to prepare for at the University of Illinois? Answering imbecilic questions? Does this warrant the debt I'll be carrying, probably for years? Especially given the salary here—or anywhere, really. I should have done that online degree like everyone said. I should have—

"You'll get better calls soon," Margo says, as if reading my mind. When I look up, she's pinned me with her sharp blue eyes. I feel exposed, like she can see right through my confident façade to my quavering, disappointed, and semidepressed core. But she can't, of course; I'm telling myself stories. And I'm done with those, aren't I? Done with making things up. "Yes," Nasrin agrees, nodding her beautiful head. "You'll get better calls soon." They're lying, but at least they're being nice. Walking back to my desk, I resolve to just deal with it. If my job is going to be answering inane questions, then so be it. I'll still be providing a service, won't I? I'll be helping those the digital revolution has left behind, just as I discussed in my master's thesis: *Digital Library Services: Tools of Equity in Community Outreach*. I could laugh now, remembering that lofty piece of work, its vision of libraries as state-of-the-art resource centers for impoverished communities and at-risk kids—not for old ladies who wanted to watch TV. But even when I wrote the thing, excited as I was by the equalizing potential of digital library services, I was always more excited by their *potential* than by the idea of applying them myself. What I wanted more than anything was to be left alone to write the book that's now a killed thing in a drawer.

But that's behind me now, so I will sit here helping old

ladies watch TV and looking up numbers for customer service. I reach my desk in a state of accepting calm, prepared for all the silly calls.

Bring them on, I think. *Send them to me, universe.*

But there's a long lull after that. No phone calls, and no one stopping by in person, either. It's late morning, so there are few patrons, but I still sit there expectantly, waiting for someone to ask about a book, or a project they're researching in their free time. But there's nothing. Nothing for *me*; the circ desk, on the other hand, is a hive of activity. Margo and Nasrin seem to know everyone who comes to the desk. I envy their busy popularity. I have no choice but to go back to scrolling through the library's website. For a while, I dutifully take notes on the electronic resource collection in the notebook I've brought from home.

These used to be my writing notebooks. Black-and-white marbled, college-ruled composition notebooks. I would fill them with lines of blue, black, or green ink, loving the sound and the feel of my pen lightly scratching the paper. Then I'd go back with my blood-red pen—a favorite Bic Roller Glide—and brutalize those lines, words, and scenes, feeling shame at what I'd first recorded but still a kind of pride that I'd done it at all. That I'd dared it. That I was doing it: *being a writer.* I filled up six of these notebooks with the first drafts and revisions of my novel. I couldn't bear to toss them after the Great Rejection, so I locked them up in my desk drawer, too. They were part of the book, after all: tainted, but cherished. Sickly cherished. I feel a little queasy looking down at the page now, even though it's filled not with fiction but with perfunctory notes: *Academic Search Premier and EBSCO Host available. Need more business resources—Reference Solutions, maybe? Brainfuse could be a useful purchase, too.* I get a little whiff of strength when I read them: here I am, *being a reference librarian.* Not a selfish, self-involved writer, but a public servant. Someone with real value in the real world.

Margo laughs. I look up, pained and paranoid for a moment. But I see she's laughing with a patron. Of course she isn't laughing at *me.*

As the day wears on, I go on hearing Margo's laugh, but with less trepidation. It's a remarkable sound, rich and a little wild, like it could spiral out of control at any moment. It draws people in, and everyone seems to like her. I long to join her and Nasrin over there, which surprises me; I've always preferred to work alone. Now, though, I want what Margo has: the warmth of company, the joy of being known. *You're never satisfied.* Dan's voice pops into my head as I alternate between watching the circ desk and exploring the contents of my desk drawers. I have to call him later to tell him how the first day went. I'm already dreading it—the tension that will simmer between us as I lie and say, *Really good. Challenging, but good.*

I'm startled by a sharp voice coming from the direction of the circ desk. When I look up, I see a disheveled woman with long gray hair, wearing a yellow tube dress that might have been chic in the 1960s. Vintage, but not the good kind. I can't make out everything she's saying but I hear "metal box" and "owe money," and watch her gesticulate with manicured hands. Margo sits before her, head slightly inclined, staring at the woman as though she were a buzzing insect, minuscule and remote. She answers the woman's complaints calmly, quietly. In response, the woman weaves back and forth, growing more and more agitated. Other patrons look up—one man clearly entertained, chuckling softly; another, younger man with an open laptop and a pencil behind his ear, frowning, annoyed. Then the woman shouts, "This is the forty-fourth book of mine you've lost. I won't pay this library a cent! I pay your salary, you know, and everyone's salary here!" I'm transfixed by the way her long hair swings behind her as she speaks, commanding the stage she's created. I'm even more transfixed by Margo, though. Her face reddens as she leans over the desk and begins to speak even more quietly than before. I find myself leaning forward, too, trying, and failing, to catch the words. Whatever they are, they work. Her once-formidable assailant deflates, shuffles out. When I next look at Margo, she's beaming at Yvonne, who's stepped out from her office. Margo's reassuring her, I suppose, that all is well. And all *is* well; Margo has made it so. She's returned the main floor to its habitual state of calm.

But I'm still caught up in the drama of what I witnessed. Not the drama of the patron's anger so much as the drama of Margo's changing face: the stark look she wore when she leaned over the desk, intimidating and cold, replaced by the smooth, blank look she wore once the woman had gone. I'd seen her morph from cheerful and chatty librarian to quietly vicious defender of the rules, and back again; it had thoroughly chilled me. And now the whole scene stirs something in me: a powerful urge.

Before I know what I'm doing, I'm opening my notebook.

I flip through the pages to a clean one. My hand holding the pen pauses for a moment—as if measuring the depth of a dive into brisk water—and then begins to move, recording word after word on the page. When I'm done, I drop the pen, massage my hand, and look over what I've written:

Her face as bland as a ball of dough, with two pin-pricks of blue for eyes. She smiles and it's bracing; it embraces. Her laugh envelops the listener, too. Her face comes alive, eyes gleaming, white teeth flashing. Suddenly, she's radiant. She loves to laugh. Loves to draw people in. When the woman approaches, M is polite and smiling at first. Then, as the woman begins to rant, M's face grows patchy with red, her look darkens. She drops her voice so that only the woman can hear. Once the woman has left like a chastened dog, M's face quickly clears: the red patches fade, and then she's calm and smooth and smiling again. Did I imagine that rage-darkened face? Did I invent the whole scene? Looking at M now, restored to her former self, I would have to say yes.

Damn it. Now I've done it. It may be rough, but it's *writing. Stupid fucking writing.* That's what I think every time I look at my locked drawer, envisioning the pile of pages and notebooks there, the work that accumulated in fits and starts over seven years, the pages I crafted and polished and sent to agents: my first novel. Or—the manuscript that *should have been* my first novel. The work that, instead, was rejected time and time again—sometimes with encouraging personal notes, but more often than not with meaningless replies like *This is not what I'm looking for at this time.* As those messages filled my inbox, refuting my starry-eyed plan, I listed close to oblivion. If I wasn't a writer, who or what could I possibly be? Not Patricia, not anything. One day, I lay on the living room floor from morning to night. When Dan came home, he nudged me with his foot to make sure I was alive. *You have to get up,* he said, furious and scared. I did—I groaned and rolled over and pushed myself up, then stood, my head swimming. I went through the motions for weeks—until one day, I *really* got up. I got up and piled every page, every note-book, into that drawer. And locked it. Dan didn't say a thing—he seemed quietly pleased. Until I started my job search.

So here I am, living my clean slate—and now I've written all over it. I read back over my rough lines, hoping to feel disinterested, detached, but what I feel is that hunger I know so well, that desire to *keep going.*

And so I do. I add to what I've written: the way Margo lifts her powerful-looking arms to straighten her bun, and how she cracks her knuckles before starting to type.

I tell myself I'm just fooling around. Just passing the time. What I'm doing right now isn't *writing.*

I look up to stretch my hand for a moment, and there's Margo, staring. After a moment, she waves. She can't know what I'm doing, of course, but even so, my face burns. I drop the pen and quickly flip the page. Taking a deep breath—inhaling the faint scent of mildew as I do—I click back to the library's website. I think fleetingly of tearing out the pages I've just written. Really, I should. But I don't, and I go on not doing it. I resolve to take the notebook home, tear out the pages, and toss them in the trash. I think of the satisfying crunch they'll make in my hand when I crumple them. And then I think of all the unpacked boxes filling the new place I've just called "home"—the drab rooms with the wall-to-wall beige carpeting and stark white walls. I found it in the town's only affordable apartment complex, one of those concrete beasts left over from the sixties, with color-coded metal stairways—mine a dark green. The building reminds me of a prison, but at least I have my cell to myself; there's no more stifling couple's routine to endure, no more dinners promptly at seven, sex at ten before reading, then turning out the light. Dan will visit me here, but not for a while. So for now, I'm free. I should go home and tackle some boxes tonight, I think with a slight burst of optimism. I'll put on some music, get takeout, and organize my books.

After I toss out those pages, of course. I glance guiltily at the notebook.

When the phone rings, I reach for it. "Reference desk, Patricia speaking. How can I help you?" I've got the greeting down now and feel a little lift because of it. I sound confident, professional. "I'd like to place an order: two fried eggs, over easy, with a side of bacon and a stack of pancakes," the caller says. "Excuse me?" I answer stiffly. "I'd like to place an order:

two fried eggs—" he starts again, but I interrupt. "I'm afraid you have the wrong number, sir. This is the Carlyle Public Library." The caller chuckles for a long time. Before I can hang up, he says, "I know, miss. I was just playing with you. Can you look up a number for me? Stevenson Auto Body on Watson Ave." I close my eyes for a moment; if I prayed, I would do it now. *Please let this be the last ridiculous call. Please let this new life be so fulfilling that I can keep my writing boxed up in the shadowy drawer where it belongs.*

"Of course," I tell the caller, and then I look the number up.

I say hasty good-byes at the end of the day and drive back home. Pulling into my numbered space in the parking lot, looking up at that hulking, weathered concrete block in the early twilight, my spirits sag. I lean back against the driver's seat. Is this it for me? A silly job and a Soviet-era home? I go on sitting there, staring as the light grows dim, feeling unready to go inside. And then I see her: Margo. I know it's her, even from this distance. Somehow I already know the slope of her shoulders and the long stride of her walk. She has on a dark coat, but the bright white of her dress peeks from below the coat's hem. I watch as she turns into a stairwell—not mine, but the blue one—and disappears up the shadowy stairs. I'm giddy, suddenly, like I've seen an old friend: *Margo lives here, too.* I remember the pages I wrote today—will I really go inside and tear them up, crumple them, toss them in the trash? I feel sick at the thought.

Once I'm home, wearing sweats, sitting on cushions on the living room carpet where my sofa will eventually be, I

take my notebook out of my bag and flip through the pages—
past legitimate notes, to the part about Margo. I've had several gulps of wine, and I take another as I read. Maybe it's the
wine, but I'm certain I've captured something of who she is—
*Her face comes alive, eyes gleaming, white teeth flashing. Suddenly,
she's radiant.* I can't help feeling pleased. It seems silly now,
the idea of trashing the pages. A bit melodramatic. *I'm not
writing a novel,* I think bitterly. *I'm just playing around with
words, passing time.* I'll leave the pages where they are, hidden
among my notes.

◆　◆　◆

I'm good and buzzed by the time I call Dan. "How'd it go?"
he asks, a slight edge to his voice. I know he wants to hear
Horribly, and even though it did go sort of horribly, I won't
give him that satisfaction. I couldn't bear to hear *I told you so.*
"It was great," I tell him. "Nice coworkers and patrons. I'm
learning the place slowly, learning my role there. You know
how it goes. First day on the job." There's silence for a few
moments before he says, "I'm glad it went well." He doesn't
sound glad at all. I can hear him chewing and swallowing:
it's seven o'clock, dinnertime. I haven't made or ordered dinner yet and feel a little swoop of freedom because of it. I'm
not even hungry, I realize. "I miss you," he says then, and
sounds so forlorn that it penetrates my buzz. "I miss you,
too," I say. Can he hear the flatness in my voice? I take a big
swig of wine to wash it all down—the sorrow and tension
between us, the strangeness of the day. When the call ends
about ten minutes later, I look around at my suite of empty

rooms with a slight pang. A kind of homesickness. Not really for Dan, but for the old, familiar life. I loved our tiny Chicago apartment: honey-toned wood floors, high ceilings, antique ceiling fans, and big windows framed by long, gauzy curtains, looking out on the vibrant city street. A place full of character and light.

My eyes land on the boxes stacked against the walls. No amount of unpacking, arranging, and decorating will give this place "character and light." I'll leave the boxes for another time.

◆　◆　◆

Every morning, I wake with the vague hope that the job will surprise me: that relevant calls will come in, that people will stop by the desk with actual reference questions. By Friday, though, I've had at least thirteen inane calls, and most patrons have avoided my desk completely or given me only fleeting hellos. Now and then I've tried to approach the circ desk to chat with my new colleagues, but I always end up walking right past to the downstairs bathroom, gripped with sudden shyness as I draw closer to Margo. The *real* Margo— not the one I've been writing. Because, yes, I've gone on scribbling notes about her when I can. I record the little things she does: the way she squints through her glasses at the screen, the way she laughs with her whole body, how she touches patrons lightly on the arm or hand when deep in conversation. It's easy to capture her warmth, her cheerfulness; what interests me more, though, and what I've been struggling to find words for, is the vein of ice running through her, glimpsed only now and then. Once, I saw her chatting with a male patron at the desk. She was noticeably less friendly than usual, and then as he turned to go, she dropped the tight smile from her face and stared after him, all the way to the door. It was close to what happened with the gray-haired woman the other day; I had to reach for the sweater on the back of my chair and pull it around me.

The phone interrupts me in the middle of a note: *Her eyes bore into the back of his head. He doesn't seem to feel it, but I do.* After my greeting, a faltering voice says, "Hello?" I repeat my spiel. The caller sounds young and confused—definitely younger than my usual callers skew. "Hi, can you look up a word for me please?" First, it's *pontoon*. Then *avuncular, corrosive*, and *fecund*. I wonder, idly, when this will end, but I also don't know if I'd mind it going on. I like the rhythm we get into: She says the word, I repeat it, then I search for it online. I read the definition aloud and she says, "Mmm," each time, as if tasting what I've said. It's satisfying for me, too, feeding her these words. All at once, I feel purposeful, alert.

And then, abruptly, she says, "Thanks," and hangs up.

I stare at the phone. It rings. I snatch it up, but a gruff voice asks for the weather report. I sit there, longing for the word woman's company. I don't even want to return to my notebook, to my sketches of Margo. That phone call was *fun*. It gave me a glimpse of what I've been wanting: a useful distraction. Who knows—if I had more calls like that, or just one very long call like that, a call that lasted most of the day, I might stay away from my notebook.

It's five, and my first week is suddenly over. I drive home

past Margo walking along the road, the only pedestrian in sight. I should stop, pick her up, and ask where she lives. *Oh, you do? So do I.* But I push the gas pedal harder, my little car shuddering, and speed away. I'm not sure I want her to know we live close; is that wise, when we work together, too? Soon she'll be asking for rides every day, and while part of me perks up at the thought, the rest of me thinks: *Not yet. Maybe not ever.* I watch her solitary figure recede in the rearview mirror.

◆　◆　◆

On Saturday, I wake early and walk the river trail to its very end, on a gravel path scattered with the first fall leaves. People passing by in small groups or pairs greet me with nods and quiet hellos. I feel embarrassed at first, to be walking alone. But why should I be? It's only force of habit that makes me feel odd without Dan at my side. I smile at every passerby after that and say a confident hello. I visit the farmers' market next, filling my cloth bags with fresh produce, local honey, and a redolent bar of soap. It's lively there, and I come home feeling invigorated. Home. It's not so bad, in the light of day, with fresh air spilling through the windows. I place my sole plant—a succulent—in a sunny spot on my kitchen table and stare at it for a moment. A sense of peace comes over me, settles in my belly.

◆　◆　◆

For the rest of the weekend, I slice open boxes, arrange books, hang clothes, and unwrap dishes and silverware in something approaching a frenzy. Dan calls Sunday morning just as I'm wiping down all of the kitchen cupboards, inside and out. I freeze in place like I've done something wrong as it rings through to voicemail. By that evening, I'm nearly done; I unpack the last box swiftly, then sit for a moment on the rug in my orderly living room. This would be the perfect moment to call Dan back, but instead I stand up, stretch my legs and my aching back, and walk out to the small balcony overlooking the parking lot.

I laughed at the so-called view when I moved in, but now, with the sunset glinting off the rows of cars, it's quite dramatic. I think of Margo suddenly and lean out over the railing to see if she's there, on her balcony, too. But why would she be? And what would I do if I saw her? I draw back and look straight ahead, to the stand of trees beyond the cars. They must be what's left of the woods that were razed to make room for this hideous building. I watch as the sun sinks below the horizon, dimming the sky.

When I step back inside, my eyes land on my work bag, still in the corner where I dropped it on Friday. I haven't been tempted until now, having thought of Margo again, but I tell myself I'll just flip through the pages—that's all. I fish out the notebook and run my hands over the words as if they were braille. Of course, I can't help reading them, too, and soon I'm seeing Margo as I've captured her—in rough brushstrokes. It's hard not to grab my red pen to revise. But what would be the point? It's just been a way to pass the time, a strategy for adjusting to my new life. Starting next week, I plan to let work fill me up—library work, I mean—instead of this *stupid fucking writing*. I tuck the notebook away with the slightest twinge, and then I go take a much-needed shower.

◆　◆　◆

"Reference desk, this is Patricia, how can I help you?" I say to the first Monday morning caller. I sound fake—so cheerful and bright—but the caller doesn't seem to notice or mind. "Hello there, how are you?" he says politely. I tell him I'm fine, and he asks me to spell *phantasmagorical*. It throws me for a moment—as these calls always do—but then I straighten in my chair and say each letter loudly, clearly, as if I'm back in the fifth-grade spelling bee: "P-h-a-n-t-a-s-m-a-g-o-r-i-c-a-l." "Wonderful," the caller says warmly. "Just wonderful. Thank you so much." I glow for a moment like a praised child. It's no less strange than the other calls I've had, but it somehow seems like a good omen for the day. I hope he'll go on—like the "word woman" who called on Friday—and have me spell words all morning. But he's finished; *phantasmagorical* was his only request. We say our good-byes, and afterward, I feel the library quiet descend like a deadweight.

The minutes tick by. I try opening various files, I try scanning the website. I can't seem to settle on one task or another; I can't will the phone to ring. Meanwhile, Margo passes by with an armload of books, humming under her breath. She's so focused, I don't think she sees me. Watching her move toward the stacks, I envy her so forcefully it's startling. She has a purpose, and it's here, right here. As for me, I've lost mine, or laid it down, to answer bizarre calls and probe the dreary realm of online research tools. Margo is fully alive and engaged—while I'm placid and wilting. Not dead inside yet—not quite. But soon, I think, staring down at my empty hands splayed on my desk. At the notebook and pen, off to my right. For the first time in months, the little pilot light flares up: *What if?* What if it's worth the risk of hellish failure to start writing again—in a real way, in a way that leads to something, that doesn't allow me to say, *I'm just playing around, just passing the time*?

Before I can answer myself, Nasrin goes hurtling past, heading for the stacks. I haven't been here long, I know, but I've never seen her move so quickly. Nasrin is a drifting, dreamy type. I hear her say something—muffled—in a frantic tone, and shortly after, she and Margo hustle toward the stairs. I want to call out or join them. Instead, I follow them with my eyes until they're well out of sight.

Minutes pass. I've been staring toward the stairwell. Nothing more has happened, but then Liz, across from me at the circ desk, answers the phone and says, "What?!" She lets the receiver drop and nearly runs for the stairs. Now I'm left: the only librarian on the floor. I look around at the few patrons, all of them deeply ensconced in their screens. No one needs me, and Yvonne is out at a meeting. I'll just go and see. My heart beats hard in my chest, though I ask myself: *How bad could a library emergency be?*

Downstairs, I find Nasrin and Liz standing, arms folded, whispering together by the bathroom door. No sign of Margo.

"There's a body in there," Nasrin says when she sees me, her eyes wide as a frightened child's. My eyes widen, too. "Don't say it's a *body*," Liz snaps. "It's one of our patrons,"

Nasrin goes on, ignoring her. "She's—she's—" "We're not sure what she is," Liz interrupts. "She's definitely . . . not well. Margo's inside." I try to take all this in, but I never imagined *a body. Here? Just past this door?* "Should we help her?" I ask. It isn't what I expected to say, but it's what comes out. I want to be *in there.* With Margo. In the thick of whatever this is. "I tried to go in," Liz replies, shrugging. "She doesn't want us in there. We called 911." I nod as if I understand, that's the best we can do, but before I know it, I'm pushing open the bathroom door. Liz and Nasrin murmur objections, but I'm moving, leaving them behind.

"I told you, Liz, just leave this to me!" Margo roars, even before the door has swung shut behind me. At the same moment, the smell hits me, fills every pore of me. I think I might vomit. I'm about to rush back out when I glimpse the scene in the last stall: one pair of legs sticking out, feet splayed in shiny black flats; another pair of legs—Margo's—entwined with them but moving, feet scrambling to push up, then failing, falling still.

"Margo?" I ask when I reach the door of the stall—even as I'm looking at her, taking in the odd sight of her pressed against this other woman's body. I can't tell if the woman is alive or dead, with Margo's face blocking hers. Either way, she's very still.

"Yes?" Margo says then, her voice muffled and strained. I watch her start to struggle up again, this time persisting until she's seated. With her hair mussed and her cheeks red, she sits there, breathing heavily, looking angry and close to tears. I find it hard to look away from the sight of this vulnerable Margo, at such odds with the woman I saw, minutes ago, humming as she purposefully worked.

"What is it?" she asks, lifting her chin. I see it quivering. Instead of answering, I reach out my hand. In the pause that follows, my eyes fall on the other woman's body, travel up to her face. She's familiar, but I'm not sure why. Then I recognize her: the woman with the lost books, the one who caused a scene last week. With Margo. And now here they are—or were—locked in a strange embrace. Suddenly, I feel a large, warm hand in my own and I look back at Margo, at her living and sorrowful face. Still red from effort, with leaking eyes. "I missed it," she says, then bursts into tears. "I know, I know," I say without thinking. I pull her up, and to me, and wrap my arms around her. She melts against me and cries on my shoulder like a child. It should feel awkward, holding this woman I barely know over a stranger's dead body. Instead, I like having Margo's warm and solid bulk in my arms. *I missed it*, she said. *What* did she miss? The chance to save the old woman? The chance to apologize? To say a proper good-bye? None of this strikes me as right.

"I know," I say again, more as a desperate but empty assertion, born out of frustration than anything else. Margo pulls back and looks me in the eye. Her dark pupils expand and contract, as if she's surprised. Or relieved—is that it? As if I've given her something she needs. I have no idea what.

She's silent when we emerge from the bathroom, so I tell the others: "The woman is dead." While Nasrin weeps, Liz only nods, dry-eyed.

◆ ◆ ◆

I return to my desk, to the quiet main floor. Margo and Nas-rin resume their places behind the circ desk, Nasrin still snif-fling. Liz has offered to stay downstairs and wait for the ambulance. An ambulance can't help the woman now, of course, but they'll take away the body; *Julia Mather's* body. Margo told me her name as we came upstairs. Still, I can't think of her now as anything but *the body*. I can't think of her as that living, annoying, threadbare woman who waved her painted nails through the air and shouted about lost books and taxes just a handful of days ago.

When I hear the ambulance arrive, followed by the vague sounds of rescue workers moving around and talking down-stairs, my eyes flit to Margo's face. Checking on her, I guess. But she looks completely . . . fine. She's straightened her hair and tucked her blouse back into her pants. She bustles around, assisting patrons, easing their minds about the noise from downstairs, the flash of red lights outside. "Oh, it's just an emergency drill," I hear her say once. She looks merry as she lies.

Is this the same woman I comforted downstairs? The same wrecked creature who told me, "I missed it"?

I reach for my notebook and start to write. I record it all: the rank smell that hit me when I first walked into the bath-room; the sight of those entangled legs; Margo struggling to sit up and look dignified. I watch Margo now, busy at her station. *What happened when you two were alone in the bathroom? Was she dead, or did she die while you were in there? And how did you get over it so fast—the loss, the failure, whatever it was you "missed"?*

Tell me, I'm commanding her. *Tell me everything.*

I squeeze the pen in my hand so hard, my knuckles go white.

Margo, of course, doesn't tell me a thing. She laughs at something a short and portly woman says.

I hate her right now: she suffered a blow; she picked herself up. Now she's stepped back into her meaningful life. And she makes it look easy. It isn't—for some of us.

But she's helped me, too, I have to admit, with a glance at what I've written. I think of that pilot light flickering on, the *what if* I was contemplating before the gruesome discovery in the bathroom.

What if?

No, it isn't worth it. I have to douse the little flame.

Suddenly, Margo looks up. She smiles warmly, so warmly, at me. I think her eyes are filled with tears, happy tears, though really, how can I tell from here? It's something about how she's holding her face. A slightly quivering chin? Maybe.

I need to get closer.

II.

I Struggle Sometimes

MARGO

After the whole business downstairs, I find myself staring at my unkempt hair, sweaty face, and untucked blouse in Yvonne's office mirror. Is this how I looked, in front of everyone? In front of Pa-tree-see-ah? How could she hold out her hand to this monstrous sight? *Brave, she was very brave,* I think to myself as I tuck and smooth and tighten. My rabbity heartbeat starts to slow as Margo—Margo as she should be—looks out from the mirror. That's better. Much better. This Margo looks professional, and she doesn't dwell on the past—not even the immediate past, even if its scent still clings to her hair, skin, and clothes. She won't lift her arm to sniff it; she'll shovel the past down and under. Return to the floor. Get to work.

Work is disrupted, though, by the muffled sounds from below, by the red lights flashing through the windows. Others begin to murmur and point, but I turn for just a moment to look, noting how the cherry-red lights pop against the gray morning sky: brighter than blood, and throbbing like a heart. The sight of ambulance lights is nothing new to me, of course, so it isn't jarring to see them now. Instead, it's like glimpsing an old friend in an unexpected spot. *Hello there, friend, why are you here?* And for a moment I truly forget. I look at the lights and think passingly of old times, but I don't see anything else—not the shrouded form on its gurney, not the ambulance drivers themselves. Soon they'll be gone, and there's work to be done. Patrons are rattled and worrying us with questions. Yvonne has told us to be "vague," but I detest vagueness.

"What's happening downstairs?" a woman with gray-brown hair, cut in a severe bob, leans across the desk to whisper. Fiona, or Francine? She spends almost every weekday typing away on her laptop in the art history corner, but she rarely bothers to stop by the circ desk. I give her my best toothy smile. "It's just an emergency drill. They have us perform these now and then. 'What would you do if someone slipped and fell in the downstairs bathroom?' That sort of thing." I give her a wink as she straightens. "Ah," she says with her fallen face, and turns away. She'll learn the truth at some point, but what do I care? Better to come up with a good, solid lie than dish out vagueness. *This is for that troublesome heart of yours,* I'd tell a patient who eyed my needle questioningly. *This will help you sleep,* I told another. Those weren't lies, come to think of it.

My buoyancy slips as the morning drags on. Maybe it's the ongoing sight of Nasrin's red-rimmed eyes or the intermittent sound of her sniffling. I want to give her a good shake, but she's delicate, Nasrin, so instead I apply clichés like little bandages: *Julia is in a better place . . . She was old and infirm . . . She wasn't in pain at the end*, and so on. They're things I've said before, to grieving relatives, and maybe that's why I start to unsettle: They bring up vivid scenes from the past. They bring up how I felt, kneeling over Julia, breathing in time with her final breaths. And then: the missed moment, the failure. *I missed it*—crying to Patricia. I feel the ants going under my skin; I even scratch my arms like I could reach them. I take a turn around the monitors, looking for trouble—but all I see are job applications, e-mails, harmless YouTube videos, and religious websites. Everyone's behaving, or seems to be. *Calm down*, I tell myself. Four hours to go; I have to make it to my bath.

Once I'm seated again, I rest my eyes on Patricia: my angel in the bathroom. How kind she was! How heroically understanding. *You'll make it through the day*, she assures me. *You'll make it to the water and fire.* But then I notice she's struggling with Martin, one of our regulars, a man obsessed with computer viruses. I saw him just a moment ago, peacefully checking his e-mail. Now he stands, flustered and twitchy, at the reference desk. I could hustle over and save her from him right now, but curiosity holds me back. What will Patricia do? First, she gives him a befuddled look, then she pushes her glasses up her nose and follows him to his station, bending her elegant figure down toward the screen. She scans it. Looks relieved. It's nothing, right? A pop-up ad, that's all. Or maybe a phishing e-mail. *Don't click on it and you'll be fine*, she's telling him, but Martin isn't having it. He stares at her with those terrified eyes, asking her, *Are you sure? Are you sure it's safe?* She nods, smiles. Tells him: *Yes, I'm certain.* Returns to her desk with him still hanging on.

He seems to settle, and there's peace for a minute or two, but Martin gets stuck in a loop. He always does. He comes back, beckoning her to his screen, and the scene plays out again, the same but both of them more intense this time, more entrenched in their roles. Patricia telling him, *Yes, it's okay*; Martin telling her, *No, it is not.*

When they finish, Patricia's mouth is set in a sour line. She sits at her desk, tapping her pen against her closed notebook. Staring into space. Waiting. Sure enough, when a minute has passed, Martin pops back up, repeats his complaint, and beckons Patricia. She looks seasick. Wobbly and pale.

It's the sight of her tears that finally does it. She sits down after this third time with Martin and blots her eyes. Blows her nose. Stares blearily around, like a soldier weary from defeat but still facing her foe.

And then Martin stands up.

Before Patricia can rise, I'm over there, tapping him on the shoulder, and he's turning to me, his dry lips parting to tell me his tale. I put up a finger to shush him, lean close, and say low in his ear: "Now, Martin, that woman controls the virus that wants to infect you. If you stay away from her, you'll be safe. She *wants* you to keep asking for help. Look at her!" We both look over at Patricia's startled, wary face. It could be mistaken for an angry face, I suppose, or even an evil one; I see Martin flinch as if he's seeing the devil. "If you sit here and carry on, it won't get you, okay? But if you go over there again, even once more, she'll plant the virus in your e-mail and we will *never* be able to get it out." If Liz could hear this, she'd scold me, but look at him! He's no longer terrorized: his eyes, once popping out of his head, are droopy with sleep now. He nods and sinks down into his chair, arms hanging loose at his sides.

With one deft gesture, I've finished him. Eased his mind. I feel lighter and happier, too, after helping them both: Martin, Patricia. I turn my head to look out the window, but the ambulance has long since gone. I feel like I've channeled those cherry-red lights, beating back the gray one bright red pulse at a time.

I glance at Patricia, who's grinning. She doesn't know how I've done it, but she knows I've broken the loop, that Martin won't be bothering her again. She mouths the words *Thank you*, and I perform a small bow. When I look up, she's laughing. How could I ever have mistaken her for Donna?

I will ask her out for coffee soon, I think later, lying warm and sated in the bath. I will sit across from her and study her dark eyes. I never tire of eyes: staring up at me terrified or grateful, relieved or done, simply done. Flat and cold and filled with black—like Julia's eyes, like so many others. I drift and dream of those myriad eyes.

My bathwater has gone cool. I start to pull myself up and out, loving the way the water sloshes in the tub, and then, when I stand, how it runs down my thighs. I dry myself with a warm towel and wrap myself tight like one of the babes in the nursery, the small, squalling creatures I steered clear of as a nurse. Too much chaos and noise. They were too coveted, too; people raised holy hell when they died. Parents howling in the waiting rooms, beating their heads and fists on the walls. There was none of that with adults—unless they were well-liked, beautiful, *and* young. But thankfully those were rare.

I feel restored after the day's tumult. And I've earned a treat, too, so I unlock my bottom desk drawer and pull out my scrapbook. Curled on the bed, looking through my collection of patient intake forms, I'm soothed and uplifted by the poignant details of my former patients' lives: second endometrial cyst removal, 2004; family history of diabetes 2; chronic abdominal pain; lung cancer diagnosis, 2009. There's nothing left of these bodily troubles but traces on paper. It feels like a kind of miracle—one that Jane orchestrated herself. When I've soaked it all up, I close the book and hold its fullness against me. It's mine. I made it. I photocopied each form, found obituary pictures to clip to the front when I could, then hole-punched and filed each page alphabetically. Opening the album again, I find no curled edges, no crinkled paper, no ragged holes. All is well in the world of the book. Finished. Perfected. No missed opportunity can take that from me. I fall asleep with it beside me on the bed so when I wake up, it will be the first thing I see. I don't believe in wallowing in the past, but this is different from wallowing; this is feasting my eyes on a work of art.

◆　◆　◆

A handsome Black man wearing a dark gray suit walks through our door the next day. He removes his hat and tips his head back to take in our high, arched ceilings, as if he's stepped into a church. I like him for that, and the way he looks around approvingly. But when his eyes land on mine, the clamping in my gut says *detective*. He smiles in a way that's meant to be disarming, but detectives always smile; they're taught to charm and also to lie through their straight white teeth. You're still a child but they offer you coffee, and then soda, which you accept, and as you sip the fizzy drink they ask, *Did you wake up and smell smoke? Or were you already awake? You can tell me, honey. If you were asleep, how did you get out so fast? Did you check your mom and stepdad's room before you ran out?* They look deeply sympathetic as you give your answers, they look at you like they're your father, almost, like they, too, left people burning behind them, like they, too, feel grief right down to their tiptoes.

They don't, of course—and neither do you. But they're too thick to notice.

I pull my shoulders back and straighten to my full height so that when he reaches the desk, I'm staring down at him, down at his shiny bald spot, down at his deep brown eyes, lifted to mine. He has stunning thick lashes and eyebrows. He holds out his hand; I take it. Patricia and I are the only two staff members on the floor, and she's over at Reference, absorbed in her work. I'm not sure where the others have gone.

"Detective Parson, CPD," he says, flashing his badge. "I understand you had a—a death on the premises here yesterday?" He has trouble saying the word, *death*, as if he isn't used to saying it aloud, here in quiet Carlyle.

"We did. Down in the ladies' restroom," I tell him. "How awful. I'm terribly sorry about that," he says, so mournful, as if he knew her, as if he cared for her the way we did. With narrowed eyes, I watch him fumble to retrieve a small notebook from his back pocket. He pulls a ballpoint pen from there, too, and holds it poised over the paper, ready to take notes. "Was that the first time you've—encountered such a thing here at the library? Or has it happened before?" I nearly snort. As if *this* were a hospital, with patrons dying all the time! I keep my face straight and tell him no, nothing like that has ever happened before. He nods and scribbles something down. *No prior bathroom deaths*, I suppose. "And what's your name, ma'am?" He smiles a little to encourage me. "Margo. Margo Finch. I work the circulation desk here. If you'd like to speak to our director, I can try to find her for you," I say, glancing around for Yvonne. He assures me it's all right, that he's happy to speak with me, but what I hear beneath the words is: *I came here to speak to you.* It can't be true, though, can it? I hardly touched her until she was almost dead. But I touched her, didn't I? And, somehow, he knows it.

We grin at each other like fools.

Beyond the detective's head, I see Patricia look up. She can't hear what we're saying but she's clocked the tension, recognized that he isn't just a regular patron. I'm sure of it.

"So, I was told that Ms. Mather got into quite an altercation here not long before her death. A day or two before, is that correct?" He blinks at me, and I answer him as lightly as I can. "Oh, Ms. Mather was always getting into altercations. Bless her heart. She accused us of losing books that she lost herself. We all loved her, but she was a piece of work, Detective. A real piece of work. We will certainly miss her," I say, letting my voice break and my bottom lip quiver. The detective doesn't falter. "Will you?" he asks. "Sounds like she was a pain in the ass." He gives a low laugh—he's my confidant, my friend. "Well, she certainly was. But we treat all of our patients with respect," I say, a little crisply. I see him do a double take and think, at first, that he's been startled by my tone. "Excuse me?" he says, his eyebrows arched. I realize it then: I said *patients*. My god. "Patrons!" I nearly shout. "I meant patrons, of course. Sometimes it's hard not to think of them as patients, poor souls!" I laugh so heartily that it fills the whole echoing room. The detective looks down in sudden discomfort, his smile frozen in place. His hand frozen over the little notebook. One or two *patrons* look our way. I can feel the heat in my cheeks but I hope Detective Parson chalks it up to that strange but innocent slip of the tongue. What else would it be? Why else would this small-town librarian be so flustered?

Unless he knows. Unless he has the whole truth on the tip of his tongue.

Ms. Finch, you're that killer nurse, Jane Rivers, aren't you?

When he speaks next, I jump.

"So, Ms. Finch, did you have an altercation with Ms. Mather shortly before she died? And were you also the person who found the body?" I'm relieved to hear him ask *this* question and not the other, even though it means one of my coworkers reported our fight to the police. Probably Liz. Of course it was Liz. I decide to answer the second question first—to correct his misinformation. "I didn't find the body," I tell him. "My coworker Nasrin did." "But you . . . approached the body, didn't you?" he presses. I think of what I did as *approaching the body* and nearly laugh. "I did. I tried to help her. Should I have left her there instead?" I tilt my head to the right. He doesn't respond to this slight challenge, though; he just keeps pressing. "And did you fight—or argue with her? A few days before?" "I did," I say calmly. "But our disagreements were regular as rain, Detective! And didn't bother me one bit. You can ask anyone," I say, looking around. Again, there's only Patricia, who can't vouch for my history with Julia. I watch the top of her head, bent over her notebook, and feel a wave of tenderness. *She* would never call the police, never tell what she saw. And she saw more than anyone.

"Look, Ms. Finch, I'm just following up on the . . . incident. There were some questions about what went on down there—" "She died!" I say, and he stares at me. I sounded too shrill, I know. "She was old, and she died," I say more softly. "I don't really understand all this fuss." He doesn't respond, not at first. Then he clears his throat. "It looks like a natural death, Ms. Finch. We're just—being thorough. I'm sure you can appreciate that on behalf of one of your *patrons*?" I can't tell for sure if he's leaned on the word *patrons* or if I've imagined it. I nod and grab a tissue from the box beside me. It's the generic kind, rough to the touch; I feel a moment's irritation with Yvonne for ordering such cheap supplies. "She really will be missed," I say, dabbing my eyes. "It's the troublesome ones you miss, you know, Detective? At least that's the way I feel."

Detective Parson's face goes soft with what looks like genuine sympathy. Even so, I don't trust it. He turns his hat in his hands and looks off toward the fiction stacks. "I'm sorry for your loss, Ms. Finch. And I thank you for your time." And just like that, he's gone, striding toward the back stairs that lead to the restroom. More "thoroughness," I bet. He'll knock first, call out, "Police," and then he'll step in and scan the tile for clues. Futile, of course. But I envy him. I haven't been down there once since it happened. I haven't stood in the last stall, reliving how it felt to have her thin hair under my palm, to see her chest rising and falling, rising and falling, but so slightly that only a terrifically watchful nurse would comprehend.

I will go down there myself, when he's gone.

No, I will not.

I catch Patricia looking my way, her gaze full of questions. *Who was he? What did he say?* But she doesn't come over to ask; I respect that. After a moment, she turns back to her screen and goes on working, as do I.

Within minutes the others return, carrying matching cups from Fresh Brew Café. I've been processing books from the returns bin. I pause and look up. "The police were here," I say drily, certain they already know. Nasrin and Liz make mild, phony sounds of surprise; Yvonne doesn't bother. "I'm sorry if they caught you by surprise, Margo. They wanted to ask you a few things about Julia, so I thought we'd get out of their way," she says, lifting her cup. I realize then that *Yvonne* must have told the police about what happened with Julia. Better her than Liz, who would have taken perverse pleasure in telling them. She has a perverse look on her face right now, relishing the thought of the detective's visit. "Oh, it was nothing," I say, waving my hands at them. "Just some run-of-the-mill questions about the whole affair. And about Julia. How we all felt about her, and so on. I told him we felt she was a pain in the ass!" I start to laugh at this phrase I've borrowed from Detective Parson but Nasrin gasps; Yvonne squints as if I've pinched her. "I hope you didn't say exactly that, Margo." I catch myself, recalibrate: "No, no, not exactly. Of course not. I said we'd miss her. Poor soul." Then I sigh, and make my face sorrowful, and tears even come to my eyes. Because I *do* miss her—suddenly, forcefully.

I miss the her I met on the bathroom floor, the one I couldn't ferry into the light. *I missed it*, I said. And meant it. So deeply, so painfully, that it nearly doubles me over now. My three coworkers stand before me in their half-hearted semicircle, muttering kind words as I cry.

After a while, they drift away. To hang up their coats and settle back into the rhythm of the day. Yvonne didn't include Patricia in their little outing, I realize—maybe because she's already "out of the way" at the reference desk. Regardless, both of us missed the field trip to Fresh Brew. And both of us, I think, deserve coffee and a chat. I blow my nose and wipe my eyes before walking over to Patricia. She looks up, quiet and still, with her pen in one hand, her other hand covering the open page of her notebook. "Would you like to get coffee sometime?" I ask. She nods and says, "I'm free tonight. Just after work?"

♦ ♦ ♦

In the café, Patricia and I smile shyly over our steaming cups. I tell myself I should sit with the silence—not rush to fill it— but I can't. When I open my mouth, the usual lies come tumbling out: I moved from Indianapolis; I used to work at a small branch library there; I visited Carlyle, found it a charming contrast to the city, and decided to move here; I've never regretted it; I've been here two years (that part is true). I expand on the usual lies, too: I tell her I was engaged to a fellow librarian back in Indianapolis, but we ended things before I moved. I tell her I fell in love with libraries as a child, when my doting grandfather took me to our local branch every Sunday. I conjure the cozy childhood I never had—two brothers, a sister, and a family dog. I tell her the dog's name was Gonzo—and laugh. She laughs with me, too. Then I look her in the eye and say, "There's nothing like a bath. Don't you love to take baths?"

It was the giddiness of all those lies, the little mountain of falsehoods I made. It forced this strange truth out of my mouth, and now I can't take it back. How loony I sound, going on about baths!

She's kind, though, Patricia—which I already knew. "I—I don't really take baths," she stammers. Looks down at her cup. I laugh again and hold myself back from patting her hand. "No, of course you don't," I say, wiping my eyes. "Listen to me, talking about baths. Tell me something more interesting, something about yourself."

I sip my tea and smile encouragingly. She looks like she's

carefully choosing her words. Or maybe she has nothing to say—or nothing she wants to share. "I'm not sure I like it here," she says at last. It isn't what I expected, and it cuts me—just a little. My beloved town, my refuge. I see what she sees out the window, though: a parking lot, a drab dentist's office, cars going by, a few trees on the roadside, and nothing much else. "You have to give it a chance," I say softly. "When I first moved here, I was thrown sideways, too. I missed the busy pace of city life. I missed my friends and my ex-fiancé. I didn't like the slow days at the library, or the weird calls." She's nodding along as I catalog *her* sorrows—not mine. Not mine at all. But I've hooked her. I tap my finger on the table to emphasize my point. "But I changed. This place changed me—for the better. Still, I struggle sometimes." *True enough*, I think with a flash of Julia Mather's face up against mine. *Yes, I struggle sometimes.*

"Who was that man?" Patricia blurts, breaking the silence that follows my little speech. "Was he a cop? Was he here about Julia—the woman who died?" She sounds so different from the woman who mumbled, *I'm not sure I like it here*. She sounds curious. Forceful. I nod slowly. "He was. He was here to make a mountain out of a molehill, like they always do. What a waste of town resources, sending him to investigate. Investigate what? An old woman in poor health died on the toilet—where's the mystery in that?" I shake my head back and forth, turning my half-empty cup in a circle. "I suppose her family wanted closure," Patricia suggests. I shift in my seat, take a hot gulp of tea, and tell her Julia had no family, as far as I knew. As far as any of us knew. She'd inherited one of the old Victorian mansions in town from an aunt and lived there alone. She had money, at some point, but it was long gone, and there were rumors of hoarding. "Not rumors to *us*—we knew she was hoarding our books," I say with a laugh. "And I doubt we'll get them back." I'm still shaking my head over this when Patricia says, "What were you doing down there? Why were you *with* her?" It takes me a moment to understand—to realize what she's really asking: *Why were you on top of her?* "It seemed like you were trying to help her," Patricia says before I can think how to answer, her dark eyes holding mine. "Yes," I say, overwhelmed by her understanding, her insight. I lean close to her over the table and tell her: "I used to help people all the time. I used to be a nurse."

◆　◆　◆

Back at home, I rummage through the drawer for kitchen matches, collect wads of paper from the recycling bin for kindling, and pull out my scrapbook. I won't burn the whole thing, of course, but I may have to burn a page or two; I'm running out of other mementos. As I'm crunching through the leaves toward my usual spot, I think: *Idiot. You had to open your mouth. You had to blab.* But I stay focused on my task. The wood is nice and dry and the fire sparks, catches, and flares up with little effort—at least there's that. *Idiot.* I pick up the album and page through it, looking for someone I can stand to part with. I only need one. Donald Jameson? No—I remember the strength of his hands, how he gripped my arm before the needle went in, how my knees went weak when I thought he'd best me. Sally Morris? No, not Sally, either. So young and sweet; she closed her soft brown eyes like a doe in the wilderness. I flip through the book twice as firelight leaps across each page. The old widower? The female judge? The distracted father of five? *No, no, no,* I think, growing more agitated with every page I turn. I can't part with any of them. I look down at the clothes I'm wearing, hoping there's something from the old life I can toss into the fire. But these are all Margo clothes, down to my underpants. I page through the album one last time, pausing at the photo of a woman with a cloud of white hair. *Janice Newington, 1963–2010,* it says. I remember Janice fondly, but I remember her bitchy daughter more. She once chased me from the room—for doing my job! For being kind and attentive to her mother, for leaning close to her as I massaged her aching limbs. I rip out the form with its paper-clipped picture and hang it over the flames, staring at the kind woman's face until the moment I let it drop. It burns quickly, consuming her smile. There. I've done it. She didn't deserve it, but it's done and I've made my sacrifice.

I stare up and around, look back through the trees toward home. There are lights in most windows, but only at one is a lone figure standing, staring out. Whoever it is can probably see the fire. I set the marred album down gently in the leaves and begin to stamp out the flames. Sorrow creeps into me as I walk back, clutching the album to my chest.

In the bath, I recall how Patricia searched my face, and squinted a bit, when I blurted out that I'd been a nurse. I wonder what my own face looked like: shocked, afraid? Right afterward, her prying questions began: "But how were you a nurse? When did you train as a nurse?" she asked. "Oh, it's ancient history," I said, waving my free hand at her as my other hand gripped the teacup. "It was my first career, right out of school. I'm old, you know?" I laughed then, hoping to distract her, hoping she couldn't tell I was scrambling to cover up. She went on staring, her face unreadable. Just a moment before, I'd felt so close to her, so moved by her understanding. But now my wariness rose like a wall. "And then you . . . quit?" she asked. I could have said nothing. I could have made up something about burnout or being called to this gentler life. But the memory of what had really happened piqued me, as it always did, and I couldn't stop myself—again—from sharing a little truth. Just a pinch of it. "Yes. I was pushed out . . . by ridiculous hospital politics," I said, raising my chin. Patricia seemed to lean closer. "I left without notice, in the middle of a shift." She stared at me. "Really? You just walked out?" I laughed and shrugged, hoping to seem nonchalant. "Trust me, they deserved it." Patricia nodded, looking thoughtful. I could tell she was formulating more difficult, delicate questions, like, *Why exactly did you quit? And why make such a dramatic exit?* Instead, after a minute or two of quietly sipping our drinks, she asked if I'd told the detective about my history as a nurse. Bile rose to the back of my throat. The very thought of it made me realize how reckless I'd been to confide in her—in anyone! "No," I said, shaking and shaking my head. "It's private information. My past. I've hardly told anyone. Please—keep it to yourself. I just felt I had to tell you—since you caught me trying to nurse someone! So to speak!" I tipped my head back and laughed my biggest laugh, and eventually Patricia joined me. But I couldn't be sure she was laughing wholeheartedly. I couldn't be sure of anything, now that she knew. Well, she knew *something*—not everything, I reminded myself. Still. She knew too much. I tried to let the laugh cleanse me, to let it clean out my fear. But the fear stayed stuck inside me and sits heavy in my belly even now, after the fire, adrift in the warm waters of the bath.

◆ ◆ ◆

The next day, at work, Patricia is the same as ever: head bent over her notebook, scratching her pen across the page. It's as if our coffee date never happened at all, a thought that equally soothes and annoys me. Shouldn't she be catching my eye? Showing she understands that I bared my soul, that I'm trusting her with my secret? Instead, as I go about my tasks—wiping down tables, pushing chairs back into place with my hip, pausing to help a clueless computer user attach a document to an e-mail—I feel her eyes on my back. But even if she's watching me, suspecting me, who would she tell? She keeps to herself. Except for that notebook. Maybe she spills it all in there: what I was, what I did in the bathroom. Well, fine; notebooks can't talk, they can't spread malicious gossip and get you fired.

I get lost in the day and lose track of Patricia—though she rarely moves. But sometime late in the morning, after a flurry of checkouts and chores, I look up to find her gone. I assume she's in the bathroom, but minutes pass and she doesn't return. After so many months of seeing the reference desk empty, it now looks odd without her sitting there. I grab a stack of books from the returns cart and tell Nasrin I'm off to reshelve. She nods and gives me her wan smile. Of all of us, she hasn't quite recovered from Monday.

I walk by the reference desk first. Patricia's sleek black jacket hangs over the seat back, her monitor is on, her notebook is closed, and her fancy-looking pen rests diagonally across it. So, wherever she is, she plans on coming back. I sweep my eyes around the room, landing on the section of reference books. She could be picking her way through the collection—Yvonne said she would be weeding it—but there's no sign of her there, among the *Blue Books*, encyclopedias, and dusty sets of town records.

Next, I try the stacks.

A–D is empty of Patricia. So is E–H. I'm beginning to think she's left the building when I cruise past I–L and spot her with her hand on the spine of a book, just holding it there, smiling as if sweetly reminiscing. I'm taking note of where she is, of where the book is, and the slim black of its spine, just as she looks up and says, "Oh," and drops her hand. She looks like I've caught her stealing. "I was just browsing," she says, a little awkwardly. I step closer, pretending to run my eyes randomly over the shelves but really locating the spot where her hand was a moment ago. The author's name: Jackson; the title: *We Have Always Lived in the Castle*. Hm. Odd. I don't think I've come across it before. "We have a good collection," I say, mimicking what Yvonne has always told me.

"Especially for such a small library." Patricia nods but casts a doubtful eye toward the books. "It could use a good weeding, though. How often do you do it?" she asks. With a defensive edge to my voice, I tell her we all pitch in to weed twice a year. What does she know about the health of our collection? She just got here. I open my mouth to say more, but she's already leaving the stacks. I get a whiff of the light, spicy scent of her skin: a high-quality perfume, sparingly applied. I approve, even in my state of slight annoyance. I've choked on many a perfume, sometimes here but especially back at the hospital. Some patients would go on dousing themselves in scent as they lay in bed in their ass-baring gowns. It felt like normalcy, I suppose, like they were still in control. It wasn't always perfume, either; sometimes it was lipstick and rouge, or an obsession with doing their hair. The men were vain in different ways: they'd touch or grab, make demands or flirty comments. I'd chuckle and think how sad they were, these men. *Just let go of all that, of who you were. It will be so much easier*, I wanted to tell them.

I always thought, if it were me in the bed, I'd be naked and scentless. It would feel so *good*—to put my life in someone's hands. To be handled and bathed. To be healed—one way or another.

Once Patricia has gone, I set down the books I've been holding on an empty shelf and move to the one she touched, the novel by Shirley Jackson. The cover shows a slim, forbidding woman in a checkered dress against the background of a pink-and-blue sky. She stands behind a locked gate with vines climbing up its bars, her face partly shadowed. A handwritten sign on the gate reads: NO TRESPASSING/PRIVATE. I like it. It gives me a cool shiver—something I didn't know books could do. Of course, I haven't opened it and don't intend to. I just want more time with it, with the cover, I mean, so I slide it under the stack of books I have to reshelve and go about my business. At the circ desk, I slip the book into my purse without even checking it out. If I did, I'd risk having to hear Liz's commentary. *You're reading a book?! Why this one? Shirley Jackson? Yes, she's odd. Very odd. I've never read her myself.* Because of course Liz will know who she is—she always does. When a patron comes in looking for something to read, Liz rattles off a litany of titles, of author names, or sometimes she leads the person right to a shelf and puts books in their hands—like it or not. It seems pushy to me. But some people love to be led, and they come back for more. *Is Liz around?* a bookish-looking man will ask. I give him a tight smile and find her for him. We all have gifts to offer up—even Liz.

At five, I walk home more rapidly than usual. I hardly notice the grass and fallen leaves beneath my feet, the sound of cars rushing by. I can't understand why I'm rushing, too. So I can get home and look at a book? But I remember Patricia touching its spine, the reverence I saw on her face. And I felt something, too, when I stared at the picture; I need to figure out why.

At home, I bathe quickly, prepare a light meal of leftover soup, and sit down with the book while I eat. I set it beside my bowl and stare at the ominous cover, at the single visible eye of this unknown woman—the heroine, I guess. NO

TRESPASSING/PRIVATE. So this woman has a secret. I turn it over to read the back:

> Merricat Blackwood lives on the family estate with her sister Constance and uncle Julian. Once there were seven Blackwoods—until a fatal dose of arsenic found its way into the sugar bowl one terrible night. Acquitted of the murders, Constance returned to the big old house, where Merricat protects her from the curiosity and hostility of the villagers. Their days pass in happy isolation until cousin Charles appears. Only Merricat can see the danger, and she must act swiftly to keep Constance from his grasp . . .

While I was reading the description, my pulse sped up. I didn't know a book could do that, either. I flip the book over, open to the first page, and start to read: *My name is Mary Katherine Blackwood. I am eighteen years old, and I live with my sister Constance.* I like her right away, this girl called "Merricat." And I like the first lines. I feel welcomed right in as she tells her story in her simple, charming way. I go shopping with Merricat in town, I bristle over the villagers' cruelty and coldness, I return with her to the safety of home, to her beloved sister Constance and charming Uncle Julian.

When I look up, fifty or so pages in, it's past nine o'clock. My unfinished bowl of soup has gone cold.

It takes an effort for me to close the book and set it aside. To drag myself up from the chair to clean my dishes and ready myself for bed. To not touch the book again when I'm tucked under the covers. To turn out the light.

In a dream, I lie on soft grass, blinking up at a circle of hostile faces. They're vaguely familiar: almost Donna, almost Liz, almost one of my old patients. All their mouths are moving but I can't hear what they're saying, and I can't respond. I can only lie there, flinching under the weight of their scorn.

I wake with a headache, wondering if reading is more dangerous than I thought.

◆ ◆ ◆

It's a troubling day at work, possibly because of the book. I feel detached from the real world, *disappointed* by the real world. It starts when I walk through the door and catch a whiff of mildew. I've never smelled mildew here before. Is it a new smell, or has it always been there and I've failed to notice? But it isn't just that: my coworkers seem flat, two-dimensional. Nasrin is a cardboard cutout, too soft and beautiful to be real. Liz is every inch the fussy librarian: short with the patrons, patronizing to everyone. And I'm none too generous with the patrons myself; when a woman with a cane steps up to the desk and asks, politely, if I could take her downstairs, I feel like rolling my eyes. I do it, of course, but I don't smile or make chitchat as the elevator carries us down. And, later, a skinny, scowling man can't find the button to turn on his computer. *Figure it out*, I want to snap. I can't help casting irritated glances at Patricia, who started all this by touching that book. By showing me that she loved it. And now she sits there, oblivious. Diligent and focused on her mysterious task. I have half a mind to walk over and tell her how perturbed I am today, but I hold myself back.

One patron—a stocky man with a shock of white hair—comes in wearing shorts, short boots, and black socks pushed down around his ankles. The bare flesh of his legs is pink with cold, but he strides in just as if he were properly dressed and takes a seat at one of the computers. He's facing me, and I make a point of giving him a sour, disapproving look. It's the thought of what I might see under the desk that sickens me: hairy flesh marked by age and exposure to the elements.

He burps. It's a long, low noise, and too pronounced to be something that slipped out. No, he *pushed* it out, proud as a bullfrog, perched there with his bare legs spread. I close my eyes against the sound. I was used to the expulsion of gas in the hospital, of course, but gas *belongs* in a hospital. It's *forgiven* in a hospital.

The smell of his burp—acrid and meaty—wafts over to the desk. I jostle Nasrin with my elbow, but she looks up, clueless.

He does it again. Louder this time. Without moving, without mumbling excuses or covering his mouth with his hand. Nasrin hears this one; she lifts her eyes to mine and laughs her softest laugh. I can't stand the sound, I can't stand her reaction. I hustle over to where he's sitting, bumping my hip hard against the edge of the circ desk in my hurry.

Across the way, Patricia flinches as if she's hit the desk herself. It fills my sails to know she's finally watching.

"Do you need the restroom?" I ask, standing with my hand on my sore hip, staring down at him through my reading glasses. He looks up defiantly. Angrily, even. That I have the gall to bother him, to interrupt his intense Internet searching, or his résumé building, or even his indulgence in gas. "I wouldn't go here if I did," he says back, looking straight into my eyes. "Excuse me?" I say, even though I've heard him clearly. "I said I wouldn't go here if I needed the restroom. I value my life too much." He delivers this with the nastiest smirk. I could tussle with him, but I feel deflated somehow. I make a small, dismissive noise and turn my back. I ignore him until he leaves, thirty minutes or so later. Barbaric, ugly man. In his shorts, baring those hideous legs. I could have told Nasrin what he said, turned it into a joke like Friday Guy, but I smile blandly into her expectant face and hold my tongue. Let her entertain herself for once. Meanwhile, I let the burping man's comment fester and burn like the spot on my hip when I press my fingers into it. I feel a dark purple bruise coming on.

"The library will be closing in one hour!" I belt out, even though we usually wait until the half-hour mark to announce the remaining time. I suddenly can't wait to get out, close the day, and take my brisk walk home. An image comes to me then, of the book waiting right where I left it on the dining room table, with Constance and Merricat tucked inside like patient wives. A surge of happiness wells up and I say it again, with jubilance in my voice this time: "The library will be closing in one hour!"

♦ ♦ ♦

I move through Friday in a daze, staring at the real world, the real people who stand before me and talk and move around, as if through a veil or dusty window. I have no urge to wipe it clean. I keep my mind and my inner view full, instead, of the characters—my friends—from the pages of my book. That's how I've come to think of it: as *mine. My book.* And *my* friends: the much-maligned but tenderhearted Constance; the clever Merricat, who sets fire to their house in an effort to chase out cousin Charles. And sweet but doomed Julian, confined to a wheelchair—

"What are you daydreaming about?" Liz asks, startling me. She's come up beside me and put her hand on my shoulder—an unwelcome touch. "I'm not dreaming at all," I tell her. It's true, but she chuckles like it isn't. "You've been so distracted lately. It isn't like you, Margo." Now she grimaces like I'm causing her pain. "Everything all right with you?" she asks, tilting her head in what looks like sympathy. It isn't, of course; I know Liz. She's simply curious. She wants to pick me apart like those fictional villagers. She *would* be a villager. She'd be one of the prying, hypocritical ones. *Did she really do it?* Liz would wonder, staring bug-eyed at Constance. *Did she poison her family?* If she knew what to ask, she'd interrogate me, too: *Did you really burn your house down with your parents inside? And did you kill all those people in the hospital?*

"I'm perfectly fine," I tell Liz, lifting up the corners of my mouth. "Just been a slow morning." Though it's only seemed slow through my book-induced daze. But it's true that I'm "perfectly fine." Every troublesome thing feels muted now: Detective Parson's visit, the secret I told Patricia, what happened (and didn't) in the bathroom with Julia. It's all remote and unimportant. The only thing I want or need or care about is Shirley Jackson's book. I hurry home and clutch it in my hands, staring at Merricat's one lighted eye before I delve back in.

The problem with this is that it can't go on forever; books end. I know this, of course, even though I'm not a reader. As the hours of the weekend pass, the right side of the book thins. I flip through the remaining pages, counting them sometimes. I try to read slower, to absorb each moment, each line, each word. I take breaks, too. I get up in the middle of a sentence to make tea. Then, when I return, I read the whole paragraph over again.

I can't keep delaying, though. On Sunday afternoon, I turn the last page, read the final lines. "Oh Constance," Merricat says. "We are so happy." But *I* am not; the little monster doesn't care about *that*. I'm left sitting here, a dummy with a shut book. That's it; the bubble I've been living in is *popped*, kaput, after a mere handful of days. I'm not one of the marvelous Blackwood sisters—I'm a villager, a stranger, pawing at the gate. Merricat calls them "poor strangers" in that pitying, despising, laughing tone of hers. *Oh Constance. We are so happy.*

What about the rest of us?!

I pick up the book and hurl it against the living room wall. It flops to the floor.

Later, when it's fully dark, I make my way to the woods.

I'm holding the book improperly, by one corner of the spine, so it flaps open in the wind. I ignore the noise the pages make. Like a complaining mouth, that book, but I know how to handle complainers. *I know you don't want to take these pills, but the doctor says you have to.*

I say to my book: *I know you don't want to burn up in the fire, but the doctor says you have to.* I'll be nurse and doctor tonight; I've done it before.

I sit there, holding the book. *When the flames are a little higher,* I tell myself. When the sky darkens a little more. Time passes; the fire warms my fingers and face. The flames are hypnotic—more than usual tonight. They're leaping high and the sky has fully darkened when I stand up to douse them.

It's a library book. *Librarians can't burn library books.*

I slip it into my coat pocket with a sigh and hastily clean up the site.

♦   ♦   ♦

On Monday, everyone is calm but me. The patrons sit before their screens or stand browsing the shelves or quietly waiting their turns at the circ desk. There are no burps, no outbursts; there is only the wild and erratic beating of my heart. I'm twitchy today, as flustered as I was on Patricia's arrival. If I could, I would hand myself a paper cup of pills and tell myself to *wash it down, there's a good girl, wash it down and relax.*

But I can't relax. Not with the book—the book I should have burned—burning a hole in my bag.

So I pull it from my purse and hide it in a stack of returns. Liz is next to me, but thankfully she doesn't notice. I couldn't handle Liz's ribbing today. I put the other books back in their spots first: three with skulls on the spine for the mystery section, one by Charles Dickens, and another by someone named J. M. Coetzee. I have no idea how I'd say that name out loud. When I'm left with what I think of as *my* book, I stare at the cover like it's the last time I'll see it. Such nonsense. I find the slim space where it belongs and slide it into place. Then I stand there with my finger on the spine, just as Patricia did when I saw her here last week. I feel about the book the way I felt about some dying patients. I couldn't let go—of their delicately shaped hands, of their wasted calves, of their thick black curls—but I had to, and eventually I did, but I was grudging, and I went on holding them in my heart. That's what comforts me now: *I will hold you in my heart*, I say to Constance and Merricat. With a tinge of bitterness, though, as I pull my hand from the book and back away.

I see the other Shirley Jackson books beside it: *Hangsaman*, *The Haunting of Hill House*, *The Bird's Nest*, *The Sundial*. No. It wouldn't be wise to read again; it throws me off-kilter. And really, I have no desire for any book but *mine*.

I watch Patricia, still oblivious to what she started in me. Her head is bent closer than ever over the notebook; her hand moves rapidly across and down the page. I resent her for being so industrious, so unchanged, while I struggle over here. She caused my discomfort, but I'm the only one who suffers.

After leaving the book, I'm just as foggy and unfocused as I was before. I hear questions like, "Do you have Lee

Child's new one?" as if through water, and my own voice sounds waterlogged, too, when I say, without checking, "No, we do not."

Do I have to burn the damn thing after all? Will that do it?

"Margo." Patricia stands before me all at once. It's as though she's heard me thinking of burning the book—my book, *our* book. Possibly soon to be *no one's* book. I can't quite believe she's left her chair.

"I'd love to get together again soon," she says, smiling. And then waits for me to snatch this up like it's a prize. "We could meet at my place for a glass of wine? I'm free tonight, if you are. We live in the same building, after all," she says breezily. I try not to show my surprise as she goes on. "I've seen you. Seen you walking home from work and—around the complex." *Around the complex.* What does she mean by that? She means: *I've seen you in the woods, I've seen you lighting your strange little fires.* A cold finger of terror goes inching up my neck: she *is* Donna, after all. I've been careless and now she's caught me out. Patricia, armed with her knowledge about my past and what she witnessed in the bathroom, has been everywhere, watching. Is *that* what she's been writing down?

Suddenly I'm back again at Spring Hill, with the glass doors yawning wide, stepping out into the cold, windy world. Cut loose. Riding terrified down the highway—to where? Oh, where?

It can't happen again. I won't let it. I open my mouth to

speak but then Patricia whispers, "I'd love to hear more about your time as a nurse." I nod dumbly, like the caught creature I am.

Jane, you idiot. Margo, you fool.

"Yes," I manage. "Six o'clock?"

PATRICIA

"I've got tremors in my legs and hands. See?" A man wearing a gray windbreaker and a light blue surgical mask has approached the desk, holding up a hand so I can see it shaking. I'm worried he'll lift his leg as well. "I don't know if it's safe for me to get the flu shot," he says, a pleading note in his voice. "Should I get it? I've heard it can give you the flu." I wait for a beat, knowing my role isn't to say, *Yes, you should definitely get it*, even though I want to. My role is to nudge him toward credible resources; that's all. I pull up the CDC website, but my mind turns to Margo. *Maybe you should consult our nurse*, I could say. What a shock it would give her, to lead him over there. She clearly hadn't meant to confide in me the other day; I saw her eyes widen and her cheeks flush before she covered it up with laughter, then shut down my follow-up questions with an appeal for privacy. It was odd. It's odd, too, that she left the job the way she did. *Ridiculous hospital politics*? What does it even mean? It's lingered in my mind ever since and makes me want to rush through the day to get to our happy hour. Even as I turn my screen to show the patron a bulleted list of flu shot benefits, I'm reviewing my after-work errands: I'll stop by the liquor store for a good bottle of wine and get snacks from the grocery store—gourmet nuts, crackers and cheese. I think excitedly of how the wine will warm Margo up, loosen her tongue, help me find out more about this oddly compelling woman who used to be a nurse.

Just for myself, of course, just for what I'm calling my "character notes."

Not for a novel. Of course not.

The trembling patron before me now seems satisfied with what I've shown him, though I have no idea if he'll get the shot. He turns to shuffle away. I hope he isn't like Martin—the one Margo saved me from last week. If he is, he'll be back in a minute, the same question haunting him, and the two of us will loop eternally—until Margo comes over to un-loop us with her deft touch. But thankfully this man settles in an armchair by Science Fiction, quite a distance away. He seems engrossed in a book he's pulled from the shelf, his medical troubles forgotten for now.

"It's like being a bartender," Margo said of our shared job over coffee last week. "People confess to you all the time. They tell you things they wouldn't tell someone they knew—you're a semi-anonymous sympathetic ear. And they think you might have answers. They're lonely, a lot of them—or worse than that. Desperate. Poor souls," she added briskly, taking a foamy sip. The phrase was pitying, but the look in her eye wasn't: it was gleaming and hungry. And the phrase itself lingered in my mind long after we'd said good night: *poor souls*. It sounded old-fashioned and vaguely familiar. Not just from Margo herself—I'd heard her say it before—but from somewhere else. *Poor souls, poor souls*. What was it from? When I got home that night, I Googled it. The first thing to pop up was a music video for "Poor Unfortunate Souls," sung by Ursula, the evil witch in Disney's *Little Mermaid*. The next hits were equally unhelpful: definitions of the phrase; religious sites offering instruction in prayer for the "poor souls" in purgatory. I must have read it somewhere, or someone I knew must have said it, but what, or who? It nagged at me. It wasn't just the phrase itself, though; it was also Margo's delivery. She said it as though she truly pitied those "souls," but like she was eating them up, too. Devouring them, like Ursula. Though I wasn't accusing Margo of being a witch—or of anything, really. Still, when she'd said it with that look in her eye, my skin crawled a little.

It came to me as I ate lunch in the staff room the day after our coffee date. I was sitting at the long, empty table with my bottled iced tea and my prepackaged Caesar salad, happy to be alone. I wasn't in the mood to make chitchat with coworkers who were still, essentially, strangers. *Strangers. Poor strangers.* Of course! It wasn't "poor souls" I knew, but "poor strangers." I knew instantly where it came from, too: *We Have Always Lived in the Castle*, one of my most beloved books. I remembered that Merricat, the main character, says "poor strangers" at the end of the book, pitying the villagers, yes, but despising them, too. She even contemplates eating one of the children, in a darkly comic line. Her tone carries all of that, and Margo's tone carried multiple levels, too: *Poor souls.*

That's when I decided to look at the book again, to revisit that final passage. I finished my lunch and washed up at the sink, then went upstairs to the stacks. The copy they had was a semi-battered 1980s paperback with a cover I'd never seen before. What was endlessly surprising about the book—what drew me to it time and again—was how endearing the sisters were, how tender they were with each other. Maybe Merricat was a monster—she had certainly done monstrous things— but she was human, too. Deeply human. I rooted for her from the first word to the last, even knowing I probably shouldn't. I stood in a daze, ruminating on all of this, then finally slid the book back into place, letting my hand linger on the spine for longer than it should have.

I stood there wondering if I could ever write anything as terrifying, funny, meaningful, and moving as Shirley Jackson's book—before I remembered I was no longer trying to write.

At that moment, I sensed eyes on me and looked up. I'd expected to see a wandering patron, but it was Margo, her arms filled with books to reshelve. I dropped my hand from the book and told her I was just browsing the collection—as if it were a forbidden thing, to stand there touching a book. We had a brief conversation about weeding the stacks, then I scooted past her and sat at my desk, feeling rattled and suspect.

But all of that happened days ago; I have a get-together with Margo tonight to look forward to. And, more important—perhaps—I need to work. And not in the sense of "work" as I used to mean it, when writing was work. Today I need to *do my job*, because I haven't finished my list of recommendations for our digital resource collection. Although Yvonne hasn't checked in about it, I sense a check-in coming. I'd like to offer it up before she asks, so once the trembling man is gone for good, I turn to a clean page in the notebook and begin jotting down notes.

I've been fully engrossed for some time when a noise—something like a bark—disrupts my concentration. Two women—a mother and her adult daughter, possibly—have settled at one of the round tables not far from my desk. They've scattered books and papers all around them, even at their feet. It looks as though they've been there all day, but I know they weren't there half an hour ago. The daughter makes a screeching noise and the mother shushes her. The daughter keeps on. The mother says, "Shut up, shut up," over and over, leaning close to her daughter's face, and then she smacks the back of her head so hard that the younger woman folds forward, her forehead nearly hitting the table. I gasp, and the pair of them look up, the daughter gazing at me emptily, the mother glaring. "Mind your own business," she says, loud enough for everyone to hear. I sit there burning with shame. When I turn to my monitor, the screen blurs and my fingers lie inert on the keys. It isn't just the public shaming I've had; it's also the intimate act of violence I've witnessed, and how little it seems to have disturbed my colleagues at the circ desk. They go on placidly checking out books, quietly chatting with patrons, while the mother and daughter moan and hiss and curse. Is this what awaits me in five or ten years? I wonder. An extreme dulling of the senses, a blindness to anything that ruffles the smooth surface of the day?

When the pair of them finally leave, I walk over to the circ desk. All three of them are there, on separate screens, but only Margo looks up. "Hi," I say unsteadily. "I'm wondering what—I mean, is that usual? Is there anything we can do?" Margo looks as though she's holding in a laugh, and Liz says, "Do?" like I've spoken an alien word. "For the daughter," I say. "She *hit* her. Right there, in public. You all saw." I'm gathering heat, getting worked up by their casual indifference. Only Nasrin looks sympathetic, her eyes melted pools. "There isn't anything to do," Nasrin says, shaking her head. "They're both . . . troubled." Margo's laugh finally breaks free at this. "Troubled? Yes, they're troubled all right. They're both *nuts*," she says, leaning forward and practically hissing the "s." She looked amused before, but now she seems disgusted, enraged, that anyone should be "nuts." "I wouldn't say 'nuts,' Margo, that's not right," Liz says. Margo rolls her eyes, but only I can see it. "They're both on the spectrum, or possibly schizophrenic," Liz pronounces with doctorly authority. "So we don't do anything when a patron hits someone?" I ask, remembering my brief orientation, my quick dive into the policies handbook. I'm certain I saw a line or two about whom to call in case of "violent disturbances." And what I just witnessed seemed to count as one. "We do, if it's someone else," Liz says briskly. "If it's Mrs. Ayers and her daughter, we don't." She turns back to her screen then: discussion over. "They live in a home for people . . . like them," Nasrin says gently. "They have social services, don't worry." She smiles, as if this fixes everything. "If they get really unruly, though, call the police," Margo says, sounding practical now. "The nonemergency number only," Nasrin jumps in to add. "Unless it's an emergency," Margo says, and I have to wonder: what, exactly, would make it an emergency? But I don't bother to ask.

Back at my desk, I reach for my notebook and start to write. Not notes for the website or notes about Margo, but notes for myself, about what I've just seen. To process what I've seen.

It's what I've always done after witnessing senseless, disturbing things—and this scene disturbed me more than usual because it involved a mother and daughter. How is it fair that my mother and I had just fourteen years together, while Mrs. Ayers and her daughter can go on living, indefinitely, in toxic intertwinement?

I wrote all through my mother's long illness and death, observing her transformation from a willowy, warm, and beautiful woman in her prime to a gaunt form curled on a hospital bed. She hardly spoke and ate only ice chips. I wrote about the bone-chilling cold of the hospital room and the sight of my mother's jaundiced skin against the ultra-white sheets. I think fleetingly of Margo; I never described my mother's nurses, though they must have been there, kind and purposeful, bringing bags of IV fluid, smoothing sheets, checking my mother's faint pulse. Could Margo have been as invisible as they were? It doesn't seem possible. When my mother finally died, I described the funeral in detail: my stiff black dress, the shine of the walnut casket they closed her in, my father's dry hand in mine, the yellow rose someone gave me to throw down the pit at the end of the service. Yellow for loyalty, yellow for eternal remembrance. It glowed against the red dirt down there, but I knew it would rot soon—like her. Turning to face the other mourners was the hardest part—feeling their love and pity envelop me, their hands reach out to enfold me in embraces that weren't, and would never be, hers.

I hated them all for being alive. I only wanted my mother. I wrote that down, too, and I even wrote that I hated my mother for dying. It felt good to write it all out, to get it outside of me. And it goes on feeling good—whether I'm writing about Margo or that upsetting mother-daughter pair. In the weeks since the Great Rejection, I've forgotten: I *love* to do this. I love to write. It's been the one constant in my life, and nothing can really stop me—not indifferent agents or publishers, not even a subpar full-time job.

With renewed energy and focus now, I tunnel forward, recording every detail: the daughter's long black hair and faint mustache, Mrs. Ayers's thick waist and bottom, the harsh sound of the whack . . . and then Margo enters the scene. I write her striding over, as she might have done but didn't. The mother looks up defiantly while shrinking from Margo at the same time. Quivering like a mouse. Margo leans over her and says that if she can't keep her hands to herself, she'll drag her out to the street. Margo stares at the woman for a while before walking away. There is no more smacking. There's noise, but it's subdued, and then the pair of them subside into silence. Margo has quelled them. *My* Margo has quelled them, just the way I wanted her to. I put down the pen to massage my hand and glance at her, the real Margo, serene and oblivious behind the desk.

Is that the real Margo, though? Or is my Margo, the one I've just written—mercurial and threatening—closer to the *real* Margo? The one who fought with Julia, then bellowed at Liz and Nasrin to leave her alone with Julia as she died? I can see this Margo stomping through hospital doors, too, righteous victim of "ridiculous hospital politics." I wonder what really happened to end her nursing career. Will I be able to pry it out of her tonight? I look at her tranquil face across the way, remembering how handily she veers between seeming frankness and self-restraint. She'll tell me what she wants and no more.

I turn to my computer, bring up Google, and type in "Margo Finch nurse." The chances of finding anything are slim, I know, but I'll give it a try. The first result is an obituary for a nurse from Montana who died back in 2001; next, a Facebook account for a Margo with long blond hair and a toothy smile, surrounded by four blond boys. There's a Black Margo Finch, too, who works as a pediatric nurse in New Jersey. I scroll through the remaining entries and find no matches, nothing even close.

I don't realize I'm staring at the circ desk until Margo lifts her head and gives me a look that makes me pull my hands from the keyboard. I start to fool around with things close at hand: a stack of bookmarks advertising last year's summer reading program, a rubber band ball, a stapler. I flip through a block of Post-it notes and then put it down with a quiet *thunk*. By the time I've done that, she's looked away, but I still feel as though she's stalked over here and fixed her eyes on my screen full of Margo Finch entries.

I should stop. Not only because I hear Margo in my head now, asking me pointedly why I'm looking her up, but also because I should be doing my *work*. I can't help trying one last combination in the search box, though. I think about Margo's having said she left her last hospital job midshift and type, simply: "Nurse disappears."

BROOKLYN NURSE VANISHES
AFTER GOING OUT FOR WALK

BODY OF MISSING STOUGHTON NURSE
FOUND NEAR HOLLINGS BRIDGE

DISAPPEARANCE OF TINA CHALMERS,
PEDIATRIC NURSE, REMAINS
UNSOLVED AFTER THIRTEEN YEARS

None of these is right, but I go on scrolling—down the first page, and then clicking onto the second page, scanning each result carefully, as any good reference librarian would.

A headline on the third results page, halfway down, catches my eye:

FUGITIVE NURSE VANISHES IN WAKE
OF SUSPICIOUS DEATHS

The article looks to be from two years ago . . . about the time Margo started working here. But *of course* it isn't the Margo I know; even so, I click on it and read, my finger trembling lightly over the mouse. By the end, my palms are slick with sweat.

I read it again. And again.

FUGITIVE NURSE VANISHES IN WAKE
OF SUSPICIOUS DEATHS

FRAMINGHAM, MASS. Jane Rivers, an ICU nurse at Spring Hill Hospital in Framingham, fled after being accused of possible involvement in a patient's death last Tuesday. She was found in the room of Kayla Jensen, 71, leaning over the bed and "embracing the patient oddly" as the woman seized and lost consciousness, a colleague of Ms. Rivers's described. Ms. Jensen was revived briefly but died before the night ended. The coroner's report determined she had died from an overdose of morphine; Ms. Rivers may have delivered the drug orally, and with an intent to harm.

"We suspect Jane Rivers's involvement in this untimely death, as well as in the untimely deaths of other patients," Warren Reade, the

Middlesex County sheriff, said in a statement earlier today. "Along with her sudden disappearance, and reports coming in from other area hospitals, this latest incident seems to indicate that Rivers was habitually taking patients' lives."

Family members of recently deceased patients flocked to the hospital this morning to demand more information about Rivers and her possible involvement in their loved ones' deaths. The sheriff's department has begun an intensive search for the missing nurse as they investigate dozens of potentially suspicious deaths.

"It's stunning," a former colleague of Rivers's who wished to remain anonymous said. "We called her 'Jolly Jane'! The patients loved her. You just never really know a person, I guess." Anyone with information on the whereabouts of Jane Rivers should contact the Middlesex Police Department immediately. They are offering a $10,000 reward to anyone with concrete information.

My lower jaw has gone slack; I clack my teeth back together and keep my eyes tight on the screen. The most damning detail, of course, is the description of Jane Rivers "leaning over the bed and 'embracing the patient oddly.'" I flash to Margo astride Julia on the bathroom floor in a literal enactment of that phrase. It takes every ounce of willpower I have not to stare across the room at the woman who could easily be called "Merry Margo," the woman who said she "left without notice, in the middle of a shift," and certainly could have changed her name from Jane Rivers to Margo Finch and taken up library work in a distant town to hide in plain sight.

With unsteady hands, I click on the picture of Jane. It's the only one they have, taken for her hospital ID, and shows an unsmiling, round-faced woman with blond hair down to her shoulders and blue eyes partly closed. Is it her? I look closer at the woman's shuttered face and try to imagine her with darker hair pulled back in a bun, lips spread in a smile . . . Jesus. It could definitely be her, with a different hair color and style. Her face, as I well know, is changeable: apple-cheeked and open one moment, severe and guarded the next. Jane Rivers looks severe and guarded here. My god, I'm burning up. Sweating so much I have to wipe my brow.

Margo Finch is Jane Rivers—Jane Rivers is Margo Finch! I close my eyes and take a deep, shaky breath. *Dozens.* Dozens of deaths. Caused by my new friend at the circ desk.

"It's too hot in here, isn't it?" Yvonne says, suddenly standing before me. "They start overheating the building in October, you should know." I didn't see her approaching because I can't see anything but the news my screen is screaming at me. Yvonne can't see it from where she stands, but what if I showed her, told her? *Your most popular circ clerk is a monster. A killer nurse.* Part of me thinks I should. I should ask to speak to her in private, then tell her what I've learned. But how would the whole story sound to Yvonne, free of suspicion, fan of Margo Finch? Like a lunatic's daydream. Or that's what I tell myself.

The truth is: I don't want to tell Yvonne; I don't want to tell anyone.

"I think I'll dress for summer tomorrow," I say, laughing a little and wiping my forehead. I hope that's all. I hope she'll walk away now, leaving me to my electrifying screen. There must be more articles, more updates on the search. But Yvonne stays where she is. "When you have a moment, I'd love to hear how things are going—with the database review." I scramble to collect myself. "Sure. Let me just run to the restroom . . . and dry off," I say with a laugh. If I can splash cold water on my face and look myself over in the mirror, I can manage giving her an update. I think. I don't want to, but I need to keep my job. "Sounds good. You know how to forward your phone?" I do, and I nod and say I will, though I doubt I'll be forwarding anything of note. Mileage between Stoughton and Kensington? Channel and showtimes for *American Ninja Warrior*, please?

When Yvonne leaves, I close the browser, clear my browser history—with a nervous glance toward Margo, as if she'd come over here and comb through it—and walk to the back stairs. I have to pass Margo as I do, with my mind screaming, *Jane Rivers! Murderous nurse!* "Hello there, Patricia," she calls out. Her eyes are bright like a predatory bird's over her signature toothy smile. *We called her "Jolly Jane,"* her colleague said.

"Hello!" I say, fixing a smile to my own face. I wonder if

she can smell it on me: what I know. I feel her eyes on my back as I walk down the stairs—even though she can't actually see me from the circ desk unless she's turned all the way around. I hope to god she hasn't.

In a flash, I remember: *She's coming to my house tonight. For wine and snacks.* The thought sends a searing stab of fear through my gut, followed closely by the first stirrings of something else. Can I possibly call it excitement? About welcoming a murderer into my home?

The bathroom is empty, as I hoped. I lean over the sink, set my glasses aside, and splash cold water on my face. It runs down in rivulets as I lean into the mirror, breathing deeply and staring. I remember what happened in the stall just a few feet away and wonder, *Did I witness a murder?* I walk to the spot where Julia died and stare down at the toilet, at the space beside it where the two of them lay entwined. Where I saw Margo struggling up. But she'd been called downstairs when Julia was close to death; she didn't *cause* it. She merely *coincided* with it. "I missed it" could have meant she missed *doing it*, I realize. At first I'm relieved, but then I feel two uglier things: Disappointment. Greed. *I wish I could have seen her killing Julia.* As soon as I think it, I feel my gorge rise. But I swallow it down, pat my face dry with paper towels. Staring bleakly in the mirror, I see it: I have a story now—or a story *has me*. Without willing it, I see my character sketches and notes cohere around a central spine: Margo as killer nurse, living a camouflaged life. Determined not to kill again, but tempted, so tempted sometimes.

She's a character in a book. *My* book. And like that, I

acknowledge it: *I am writing a book.* I don't deny or shy away from it this time. I can't. How can I deny a story like this? One with such power and potential momentum?

I don't think for one moment, *I should go turn her in. I should call the police.* Or—I think it, but I bat it away.

Looking in the mirror, I see a vision of myself: face clean and eyes bright, lips lifting in a smile. I'm no longer the sad, defeated person I've been, no longer the woman weighed down by those hundreds of pages, that albatross. This woman, Patricia, is *writing a book.* When I reach out, she's silken and cool to the touch.

◆　◆　◆

The rest of the day goes by slowly, so slowly, like walking through waist-high water. I meet with Yvonne and report on the fake progress I've made. I feel a distinct split inside of me as I talk about the research databases I'd like us to buy, gesturing with my hands to emphasize their potential impact on the community. She seems convinced by this performance, even as I'm quietly reliving the moment I learned the news about Margo and then the moment just after that, when I resolved to *write a novel.* On leaving her office, I feel certain I've pleased her and secured my job, but I'm depleted, too, having had to force out so much false enthusiasm. How will I make it to the end of the day and then have the strength and the nerve to sit with Margo in my living room?

I see her throughout the day, though we don't cross paths. Our eyes meet now and then, but her gaze feels light, incurious. I'm deeply relieved. She hasn't sensed me trembling at my desk, swerving, internally, from terror to giddiness and back again.

One minute I want to cancel; the next, I'm planning my book tour.

The clock creeps or hurtles forward, depending on how I feel.

♦   ♦   ♦

"See you back at the ranch!" Right at five, Margo stands in front of my desk with her coat on and her bag slung over her shoulder. "I'll see you in a little bit," I say, breezily as I can, trying not to wince under her gaze, feeling, instinctively, like I should cover myself with something, as if my body itself must be revealing what I know.

Yvonne is working late, as usual, but aside from her, I'm the last one to leave. I need to hurry to the store, but when I look for my car, I find a tall, slender man standing beside it: the detective who spoke with Margo the other day. I stop where I am as he lifts his hand and smiles. Forcing myself to take one step and then another, I walk toward him while lifting the corners of my mouth in what I hope is a confident-looking smile.

I know that Margo is long gone, but I glance in the direction she would have walked anyway. Could she have spotted him when she left the building? Could she have lingered somewhere, in the shadows, to see who he was waiting for? I have a feeling, though, that he stayed hidden until I stepped through the door.

When I reach him, I stand there shivering, realizing

belatedly that my jacket is still draped over my arm. He offers me his hand. "Ms. Delmarco?" he asks. I nod. "Detective Parson, CPD. I'm sorry to catch you here as you're trying to get home." He isn't sorry, of course; he starts right in, asking me about Julia's death. I tell him the plain facts: that I walked in and saw Margo helping Ms. Mather on the bathroom floor. I'm clear about the word; I lean on it: *helping*. He nods and scribbles. Even through my nervousness, I like him for having an old-fashioned notebook and pen; it soothes me a little to watch him write. With my eyes on his pen, I stumble through the narrative. "She was down there on the floor. She was trying to lift up Ms. Mather's head, to get her up," I say, though I know this isn't true; Margo was pressing Ms. Mather down and scrambling to get *herself* up. But the lie comes tumbling out anyway.

Detective Parson's writing hand stills; he catches my eye. I think for a moment that he knows I've lied—that he knows everything somehow. "How well do you know Ms. Finch?" he asks. I look down at my shoes, thinking about exactly how well I know "Ms. Finch" as of this afternoon. "Well, I'm new, so . . . not very well," I mumble at last. This is the moment when I could grip his writing hand, lean in, and say, *Her real name is Jane Rivers, and she used to be a nurse. Look her up.* But I don't. I shrug and offer up what little I know, based on what I've seen at work. "She's very cheerful, and the patrons seem to love her. She knows everyone. And—and she's a hard worker." All of these things are true, though I keep the kernel of the innermost truth to myself. Hunch over it, cupping my hands around it like a precious jewel.

"And how did she seem after the incident?" he asks, looking down at his notebook to record what I've just said. I'm glad he can't see my face as I remember how quickly Margo recovered, how her whole being brimmed with joy. "She seemed terribly upset. Everyone was upset," I tell him. It's getting easier to lie. After more scribbling, he flips his little notebook closed. "Thank you for your time, Ms. Delmarco. Here's my card if you think of anything else." As I take it, a long shiver runs through me, but when I meet his eyes, I smile and shake my head. "I don't think there's anything else I can tell you, Detective." "Well, keep it just in case," he replies, arching his eyebrows. He's far too beautiful to be a small-town cop and seems to know it. Holding his gaze, I suddenly ask, "Why are you investigating this like a suspicious death? It seems fairly straightforward, doesn't it—a lonely old woman dying in a public restroom?" It sounds so callous that my face heats with shame. I would try to soften what I've said, but I don't know how, and it's too late anyway; the detective's sharp eyes pin me in place. "Just crossing my t's and dotting my i's, Ms. Delmarco. It's my job." He touches his hand to his hat, says good-bye, and then walks off into the night.

What if he knows? What if he knows? the anxious voice in my head repeats. But he can't know. There's no reason he would suspect Margo is anyone other than she claims to be, and even if he thought she had some part in Julia's death, or that something was off about the incident, his suspicions would never lead him to the larger truth.

Even so, I stand frozen by my car for a moment. My keys hang uselessly from one hand; I hold the detective's card in the other. I've just lied to the police to protect a killer. I squint at the cell phone number printed on the card and tell myself I can call him later, I can call him tomorrow—I can call him *anytime*. But if I told him the truth, he would wonder why I lied; he might even suspect *me* along with Margo then. I stuff the card in my pocket to be forgotten and hope to never see him again.

♦ ♦ ♦

I'm one glass of wine in and feeling warm but still terrified when Margo arrives at my front door, bearing a bottle of cheap red wine. She tells me gruffly that she doesn't drink "the stuff" herself, and I wilt; so much for loosening her up. She even turns down tea and asks for a glass of water, no ice. I direct her to my newly arrived red couch and urge her to sit a bit too eagerly; she stays standing. When I leave her to prepare our drinks—her water, my second glass of wine—I take several deep breaths. At first, I fill my own glass almost to the brim, but then I think better of it and pour a third of it down the drain.

Returning from the kitchen, I find Margo peering down the dark, narrow hall to the back rooms. It strikes me that Margo's place and mine must be laid out identically. That we walk down the same hall to the same small bathroom, with its beige tile and bright fluorescent lights. That beyond it is the bedroom, where we stand at the long rectangular window that looks out over the sea of cars. A different part of the sea of cars, but still: the sea of cars. We see the sunset from there, or from our balcony off the living room.

Margo could be thinking the very same thing right now. I shiver, and she turns. Gives me a minuscule smile and takes her water from my hand.

"You asked about my nursing career," she says, sitting abruptly on the couch. I sit just as abruptly next to her, amazed that I won't have to prod her toward the subject and feeling a clutch of panic in my chest at not having my pen and notebook in hand. What would Margo do, I wonder, if I said, *Just a minute*, and retrieved my writing materials? Instead, I say, "I'm so curious about how you went from being a nurse to being a librarian. Such different jobs." Shaking my head as if in disbelief. Margo makes a dismissive sound at this. "Not so different sometimes," she says, sending me back to the bathroom with Julia, and then farther back, to situations I never saw with my own eyes—to hospital rooms where Jane hovered over the dying. *I am sitting here with a killer*, I tell myself, quaking at the thought. Still, I manage to tuck my legs beneath me and lean into the corner of the couch, wine in hand, encouraging her with what I hope is a relaxed smile.

Margo tells me she was drawn to the nursing profession as a child, that she knew even then it was her calling. She describes her hectic early days on the job, the drama of the OR, her intense devotion to her patients, the "Top Nurse" award she won several years in a row. She spins the story like a dream, and while part of me knows she must be exaggerating—or even lying—all of me hangs on every word as Margo, heroic nurse, graces the hospital hallways, spreading health, well-being, and cheer. She speaks of the camaraderie she shared with her colleagues, how they respected her work ethic and relentless positivity, how she assisted many a surgeon during complex procedures (and even calmed a panicking young surgeon in the middle of one), how she befriended the overworked nursing aides who suffered at the hands of doctors, nurses, and patients alike. She brings the hospital to life for me, too—its sounds and sights and overwhelming smells—and I am caught up, enraptured. I am all ears; I forget that I'm a body on a couch.

And then she stops. Sighs a little. Takes a ridiculously small sip of water, a child's sip, then places the glass carefully back on its coaster. She's reached the end, it seems, though it didn't sound like an end. It sounded, instead, as if she stepped right out of that brisk, engaging, richly layered life into this new one at Carlyle Public Library, without any fanfare or fuss. No disenchantment, no decision. Just a step to the side, and now here she is. She looks at me and smiles, as if to say: *All done.*

"But what happened to your . . . I mean, how did you end up here, at the library?" My cheeks color with the brazenness of this question I already know the answer to: She was caught in the act, exposed as a killer, and fled. Reinvented herself. But isn't this what I'd ask if I didn't know the truth? Besides, I'm eager to hear how she'll answer it, what lies she'll try to feed me.

She hasn't touched the cheese and crackers, or the bowl of gourmet nuts. I reach over from my corner and scoop up a few cashews. I'm chewing these when Margo picks up her glass and takes several long swallows of water.

In the silence, I look through the sliding glass door that leads to the balcony. The small patch of trees behind the parking lot is illuminated, just barely, by the fading light. It's more sad than pretty—the trees look scrubby and bare—but it reminds me of something I saw, something I'd forgotten until just now.

"I saw someone standing by a fire in the woods the other night," I say, still looking at the view, wondering if those qualify as woods. "Isn't that strange?" She gives me a sharp look. "Maybe it was kids," she suggests quietly, setting her glass back down. "No. It was one person. And not a kid," I add, recalling the tall, hunched figure and beginning to wonder, just now, if it wasn't Margo herself, burning evidence from her past. Maybe the Julia incident and Detective Parson's visit have made her skittish. Though she doesn't seem skittish. Not one bit. She looks at me now with her head tilted, her small blue eyes alive in her plain face. "It's not against the law," she says. "No, I'm sure it's not. It was just . . . unexpected," I mumble back. Is she daring me to ask her outright? To say, *Margo, was it you?* As I'm stumbling for ways to turn the conversation, Margo suddenly shrugs and says, "It was the other nurses." I'm confused at first; the other nurses started the fire? Then I realize she's answering my original question, and I'm relieved. I lean back against the couch, ready to return to her fabricated story of what drove her from nursing to library work.

"They were jealous. The patients loved me, needed me, preferred me to everyone else." She lifts her chin in a way that seems challenging, as if I'd deny her version of events. I *could,* of course, but I won't. Besides, I'm too busy drinking in her transformation: she's gone from charming, voluble Margo, the woman who wove me that hospital fairy tale, to combative, bitter Margo, the woman with the pinched face and darkened eyes. I've never seen her look more like that online picture of Jane Rivers than she does now. I clear my throat nervously, then hold her gaze and nod to say, *I believe you, go on.*

"I made a small mistake one day—something anyone could do, at any time. But my *colleagues,*" she says with hateful emphasis, "made it into a colossal deal and pushed me out." I know I could ask her now, *What was the mistake?* And she'd tell me something banal, like a paperwork error or a lapse in bedside care. But I've suddenly lost my nerve, sitting so close to her that I can trace the crow's-feet around her shrewd blue eyes. Instead, I ask if she couldn't have simply moved to another hospital—a more roundabout question—and she shakes her head. "I couldn't. I had no references. They'd gotten to the doctors and the administrator, convinced them all I was unfit to be a nurse. Even despite everything I'd done! If the patients had known, they would have risen up out of their beds and fought for me . . . but that's what happens when you align yourself with the weakest, the most vulnerable," she says, nodding. "You have no power, no one lifting you up. You make *yourself* vulnerable." She goes on nodding as I watch her, thinking, *And what happens when you harm the weakest, the most vulnerable? I mean, what happens in your head? Your heart? What do you get from it, Jane?* Questions that come straight from my cold writer's brain;

questions I could never ask. "I knew what was coming," she goes on. "And I knew I couldn't stop it. So, one day, I just picked up my things and left without telling anyone—like I told you before. Right in the middle of my shift." She chuckles now, shaking her head. "They must have been shocked. I wish I could have seen the looks on their faces when they realized I'd gone." I can think of nothing to do but chuckle along with her in fake appreciation of an outright lie, and then I take a deep, final gulp of my wine, tipping the glass back like a drunk. I wish I were drunk now; I wish I hadn't poured that portion of wine down the sink. I could go get more, of course, but I don't want to disturb the flow of the story, even as each word out of Margo's mouth disturbs me more.

She clears her throat, then tells me about coming straight to Carlyle from the terrible hospital ordeal, discovering this quaint town on the Platte River by chance. She says she felt a sense of peace and well-being from the moment she walked through the library door. She neglects to mention any of the things she told me over coffee: That she was lonely, that she was underwhelmed by the job. That she moved here from Indianapolis, having worked at a library there. None of that fits in her fantastical tale, so she discards it. She's Margo the Librarian now, and everything in her looks and demeanor tells me so. It's chilling: how her color has changed to a light, rosy pink, how her lips lift in a soft smile. "Now I enjoy my work every day without the pressure and stress of the hospital," she says, folding her hands gently in her lap. I smile back, but inside I'm twisting with the frustration of not being able to ask: *Why did you do it? How did it feel? Have you really stopped killing?* The writer in me sits thwarted, and with a fading buzz, while the rest of me squirms like a captured mouse.

"Now. How about you? What's the latest news in your life?" she asks with a matronly air. I'm not prepared for this shift—I've been in listening mode so long. "Oh," I say, feeling myself blush. "Um, my boyfriend is coming soon. From Chicago. Just visiting for the weekend." Margo nods her approval. "Well, that will be nice for you. You'll have to bring him by the library, you know. Thank you for having me over, Patricia," she says, rising abruptly to her feet. "Oh," I say, wanting to reach out, to stop her from going. But by the time I've stood, she's already at the door, showing herself out. *Party over.* My audience with Margo has ended—and what did it achieve? I feel deflated and slightly angry, as if I've been cheated out of something. But what was I expecting—the truth? A full confession? An airing of her innermost murderous thoughts and feelings?

It's irrational but my answer is: Yes. Part of me expected those things. Wanted them, too.

I pour myself a very generous third glass of wine and sit on the couch, staring into space, nibbling on crackers and cheese, unable to do anything else.

Sometime later, I rise creakily from my seat and see it through the window again: a small triangle of fire with a solitary figure beside it, tall and slightly stooped, just visible through the trees. Is it Margo? I squint through the darkness but can't be certain from this far away. I imagine her standing there, feeding page after page of something incriminating into the flames. My exhaustion fades, and before long I'm sitting at the dining room table with my notebook and pen, hand moving quickly to capture the scene: the fugitive nurse huddled over the fire. Someone watching her: A curious neighbor? Or a detective, hidden behind a nearby tree. Later, he'll scrape through the ash, looking for bits and pieces of evidence but finding nothing. He'll leave her alone—but not for long; her strange behavior keeps him circling around her. I look up now and then as I write, catching the glimmer of Margo's—or someone else's—fire through my reflection in the sliding glass door. When I finally drop the pen and sit rubbing my hand, I see the fire has been put out. The woods have become a wall of black beyond the parking lot lights.

◆   ◆   ◆

My ringtone startles me. It's Dan. I think about not answering, but it would be odd to avoid him at this hour. What would I use as an excuse? *I was out partying in Carlyle on a Monday night?* When I pick up, he reminds me he'll be here in less than a week. I knew that, of course, but in the wake of what I've learned about Margo, Dan's visit has shrunk to a sliver of nothing in my mind. Even so, it's coming up fast. "I can't wait," I say, thinking he must be able to hear my lack of excitement. "What will we do?" he asks, though he's never asked that before, not when we'd sit idly for hours in our tiny apartment. But I know what he means; he means: *What will we do in that boring shit-town you moved to?* "Walk the river trail, shop at the farmers' market, eat at the restaurants downtown," I say flatly, already dreading the hours I'll lose to our

tedious togetherness. "I'll have to show you the library, too,"
I add, thinking of Margo. My voice lifts. "It's a beautiful old
building. Interesting coworkers. I've told you about Margo,
haven't I?" I sound like an eager child. "I think so," he says
tentatively. "She's the one who found the dead lady in the
bathroom, right?" I start to correct him—she didn't *find*
Julia—but I let it go. "That's her!" "Excited to meet her," he
says ironically. There's a long pause, one I hope to fill with
good-bye, but then he blurts out, "Listen, are you . . . writing
again?" It jolts me. His tone sounds like, *Are you cheating on
me?* Dan was visibly relieved when I locked my novel in that
drawer and swore off writing forever. "No," I lie. "I'm done
with all that." I feel giddy, lying so silkily to him even as my
mind turns to Margo, to Jane, to the notebook and pen just
inches from my hand. "Probably for the best," he says. If I
could, I would reach through the phone and throttle him. "I
have to go, Dan. Work tomorrow. I'll see you soon." He
doesn't seem to notice my tone or pause to wonder about my
brusque good-bye. "See you soon. Love you," he says, sounding cheerful.

I sit in the emptiness and quiet after the phone call, letting my blood cool down. *Probably for the best*, my ass. But my
anger fades quickly. Before long, I pick up my pen to reenter
the beguiling world of my book.

III.

That's That

MARGO

As I told Patricia about my nursing past, I could almost see her cramming each colorful detail into her mind like a greedy child. She wanted to eat it up, the enhanced version of my former life, so I let her. I dressed it up, exaggerated, skipped some parts. I made it sound like one of those hospital TV shows, but she didn't notice or care. She was blinded by the beauty of it. The story of it. I knew she would be.

I gave her nuggets of truth, too—not that she'd ever be able to pick them out. I *was* a calming presence in the OR. I *did* talk a young surgeon down, once, in the middle of a procedure, and after that, he would have no one but me assist him. The other nurses *did* ambush me, they *were* jealous. And the patients *would have* risen up out of their beds to defend me—some of them, anyway. The ones who could still rise. I was their bright spot in the gray of life, wasn't I? I brought them my beaming smile, and when I leaned over them, locked eyes with them, I know they felt a bracing little breeze. It lifted them right out of the muddy depths. It still pains me to think of them without me, poor souls. Spinning through channels on the clunky hospital remotes, staring out the windows at the sullen urban skyline. Life without Jane would be a dreary, empty place.

My patients would have saved me, I know it. But what could they do? The nurses had circled me with their daggers out; they'd formed a pack. And then the scene I had with Donna—which I didn't share, of course—clinched the deal. Tightened the noose. She kicked out the stool and my legs swung free.

For Patricia, though, I've made it dramatic with only a touch of ugly—not the tide of ugliness it truly was. I've kept my voice airy, as if none of it really matters anymore, as if I've dropped the past behind me like an old rag. That was my aim tonight: weaving a tale to distract her from any ideas she might be getting. I had a slight scare when she mentioned seeing a fire in the woods—but why would she suspect me of that? And what does it matter, anyway? It's not against the law, as I said myself. I doubt she'll concern herself too much with that now—and hopefully I've settled her mind about my nursing career, too. It was a productive evening. When I left Patricia's, I stepped out into the stairway feeling relieved—as though I'd performed an unpleasant but necessary duty—like the feeling I used to have when I finished changing a bedpan. There was a brisk wind blowing, and it cooled my cheeks. I watched leaves scuttling between cars in the parking lot as I descended her green stairs, ascended my blue ones. Measuring each step, even though I felt like running toward my end-of-day bath.

And now I'm scalded and scoured, serene, with a purified soul. Who needs religion when you can have a nightly bath?

One of my hospitals was Catholic, and the black-robed priests who came seemed to float, footless, over the floor. There were very few times a door could be closed to a nurse, but the priest visits were one of them, and I seethed over the intimacies I knew they must have shared with my patients. *My* patients. One time, a young and very sick woman we all loved called for a priest toward the end. When he came, I couldn't bear the smug way he moved down the hall and tapped lightly on her door, expelling even her family from the room. I watched it all from the nurses' station, waiting until her husband and children took the elevator down to the cafeteria. Then I pushed through the door to her room with the blood pressure cuff in hand and her chart tucked to my chest, calling out, "Mary dear, it's time for your vitals," as if I had no idea I was intruding. It wasn't the priest's look of annoyance that fazed me; it was Mary's face, red and streaked with tears, swollen in open misery. This was the woman who would joke with us as we changed her IV or gave her pills to swallow. "You won't let me skip these, even now?" she'd ask with a grin, and we'd chuckle and shake our heads. The priest had transformed her, wrung truths from her—I couldn't stand to see it. I turned on my heel and walked right back out to sit at the nurses' station, shocked and fuming. Mary had never cracked open like that for *me*, no matter how

I'd coddled her. She'd kept up the smooth display she showed everyone else—except for the bland little man in black. The whole scene I'd witnessed felt like a betrayal, and a violation, too. I was gruff with Mary, later, when she tried to joke about the contents of her catheter bag. I liked seeing the hurt look on her face. And then, not long after, she died.

All of that praying and confessing she'd done hadn't saved her life. I could have told her it wouldn't. But the priest went on pacing those hospital halls, preying on the weak. I imagine he still paces them now.

◆　◆　◆

I was stalked by the past in sleep, and now I'm stalked by it as I sit chewing my breakfast. Last night I dreamed I was driving away from Spring Hill, just like I did in real life. The dream was nothing but driving; no one chased me, there was no fear, no urgency. Only driving, long and monotonous. Leaving behind the compacted scenery of the east for the wide, flat sweep of land as I drove farther west. Driving into nothingness, it seemed. Pursued by no one. *No one wanted you*, I tell Jane as I swallow my cereal. There was nothing, no one to stop me, not even when I pulled into a gas station and parked by a police cruiser, tempting fate. The driver and his partner looked right through me when I smiled, as if I were part of the scenery. I cried myself to sleep in the first motel room, then woke to an explosion of news. "Jolly Jane" and "Fugitive Nurse" and all the rest. Ha! I chuckled over the news all morning, then swelled with a sense of purpose. I bought hair dye and clothes Jane wouldn't have worn in a million years, they were so staunchly middle-aged: floral shirts and stretchy slacks. I stared in the bathroom mirror with my new reddish-brown hair worn up in a bun and with bangs that Jane would have hated and said *Margo* before I could even think too much about it. Margo, the name of a queen. I didn't know if it was the name of a queen or not, but it sounded like one. I would be different now; I would be dignified and restrained. I would keep heading west until I landed in a place that was worthy of Margo—and obscure enough to keep her safe. The fools from my past would never find me.

That's over now, Margo. Let it go. I brush my hair and put it up just as I did that first time, though I've grown out the bangs. I see the first glint of blond at the roots. I've been so careful, not letting it go even the slightest bit, but today I look in the mirror and shrug. No one will notice—no one examines my hair, my body, my clothes. Then I remember Patricia. Her look makes me feel as if she's turning me over in her hands, inspecting my spine and pages for wear, thumbing my table of contents. Or what she *thinks* is my table of contents. Just yesterday, I caught her giving me an intense, searching look. As soon as I glanced up, she dropped her eyes and picked up this and that on her desk. Later, I saw that she'd turned back to her screen, and her face, so vivid earlier, was petrified and gray. She looked like Donna when she'd walked in to find me perched on Ms. Jensen's bed, breathing in her death. I had turned to see Donna's face, like Patricia's but worse—paler, uglier, her mouth distended—and I'd scrambled to extract myself.

Reluctantly, I might add. Even then, even caught in the act.

But Patricia hadn't caught me in any "acts"—unless you count Julia. I do not.

Not long after, Patricia passed me on her way to the bathroom, still looking unwell. I said hello; she said hello back. Her eyes were glazed; her forehead shone with sweat. She looked like she was coming down with something, or like someone had fed her poison. But when she finally returned, she came striding by the circ desk with a generous smile, a light and happy air. She'd blotted her face, reapplied her lipstick, and looked as fresh and lovely as I'd seen her. Whatever had distressed her—boyfriend troubles, perhaps—she seemed to have swallowed it whole. Digested it. Pooped it out. *Good girl*, I wanted to say. *Good girl*.

◆　◆　◆

Today is Nasrin's birthday and she's brought homemade cookies for everyone. We can't all meet in the break room at the same time and leave the floor unattended, so at ten a.m., Nasrin, Patricia, and I make up the first shift. Nasrin is telling us about her beloved terrier—how she bought him cute new accessories for winter: a tartan plaid waterproof coat with matching booties. I'm listening with one ear but darting my eyes now and then to Patricia's distracted and dreamy face. "That dog is so spoiled, Nasrin," I say abruptly, wanting to jab Patricia awake. I've only jabbed Nasrin, though, who gives me a wounded look. "Nicely spoiled," she retorts. Her jaw is quivering and it's her birthday, so I relent. "Of course, of course," I say, smiling and reaching to pat her hand. "And I'm sure he's very cute in his little outfit." We make more mundane conversation about pets and the cost of living in Carlyle, which is higher than it should be, while Patricia sits beside us, a smile frozen on her face. She's lost in thought, though Nasrin doesn't seem to notice. Eventually, Nasrin pushes back her chair. "Well, thank you for the birthday cheer, ladies. I should go back upstairs so Liz can come down." She hesitates, waiting for me to stand and say I'll go up in her place—that's what I *should* do, after all. The birthday girl should be able to stay. But I look up at her, smiling blankly, until she goes. Patricia breaks her silence, at last, to wish Nasrin happy birthday, and then, suddenly, we're alone. She gives me a tight little smile, then looks away, twisting her neck toward the open door as if she'd like to leave. As if we're seated too close, though we were seated much closer last night. I start to wonder if her troubles are boyfriend related after all.

What's up with you? I want to ask. *And what does it have to do with me?*

Maybe nothing. Hopefully nothing.

"How are you?" I blurt. She tells me she's fine. "I'm great, actually," she adds, nodding and nodding. She looks like she's trying to convince us both. "My boyfriend is coming Friday." "Oh, right," I say, dreading the banality to come. How many times did I have to hear about patients' boyfriends or girlfriends or latest dates when what I wanted was to lie atop them and quietly search their eyes? But I do want to draw Patricia out and see if this might be the source of her swinging moods, so I have to bear with the news of the boy-friend. "Is he a librarian, too?" She gives a short laugh and shakes her head. "No. He's an accountant at a law firm." "Ah," I say, as if that's wonderful, thrilling. "How did you meet, then?" "We met at a party when I was in grad school," she says, her cheeks flushing. I don't understand her sudden and obvious discomfort. "I didn't know there were parties in library school," I say, laughing and casual but digging for more. It works. "I went to grad school for writing, before." She stuffs the rest of the cookie she's been eating into her mouth and sits there, looking miserable, as I watch her chew. I imagined she'd eat like a dainty bird, not a hunted dog. But I guess she feels hunted. She's given me something, a private tidbit: my new friend Patricia is a *writer*.

I should have guessed it already, of course, seeing her glued to that notebook. This explains the changing weather of her face, too. When the writing's going well, she looks lighted from within and slings her happiness around. When it isn't, she retreats inward, looking miserable and pale.

She starts to scoot back her chair, but I stop her. "You're a writer?" I ask. Annoyance flits through her eyes, but even so, I don't expect her forceful answer: "No." Now I'm confused. Why would she have gone to writing school if she *wasn't* a writer? "I mean I *was*. At the time. But I'm not anymore." I flash to Patricia, hunched over her notebook at the reference desk. "But I've *seen* you writing. In your notebook. And how do you quit writing, anyway? Is that even possible?" She picks up her napkin, then sets it down. Then crumples it up. "I didn't quit. I failed," she says in a dead voice. "I tried to write a novel for many years, but . . . it didn't work." She's raised her chin, as if she expects me to challenge her, but I'm too confused. "You mean you tried to write but couldn't?" She gives a wry little chuckle in response. I can tell she's not trying to guard her secrets anymore, that she's opening up, the way my patients used to. They let me pry them right open and stroke their soft hearts, their liquid organs. I won't get that far with Patricia, I know. "No, I wrote many pages— hundreds of pages. And rewrote them. Perfected them, I thought. I sent the book to agents. Tons of agents. Some of them were interested, at first, but in the end . . ." She trails off, shrugs. Tears glisten in her eyes. "I'm sorry, Patricia. That sounds terribly hard," I tell her, letting my voice break. "It is. Or it *was*. I'm—turning over a new leaf here. Focusing on this job." She nods again, too energetically. I repeat what I said before: "But I've seen you writing—in your notebook." She shakes her head, gives me a bright smile. "Oh no, I'm not *writing* writing. Those are just notes. Work notes. About the databases and collection. It's nothing." She sounds breezy now, and I do not believe her. But she's finished. She stands and wipes crumbs from the front of her skirt. "I should get back," she says, proving her commitment to the reference desk. I want to stop her, grab her arm and say I'll keep her little secret, but then Liz walks in, breathless. "Are there any cookies left?" she asks.

♦ ♦ ♦

I watch Patricia, back at her desk in the late morning light. If she's furiously taking notes about the *databases*, I'll be hanged.

She only takes a breather once—with her eyes glued to the page—to massage her hand and shake it out. Whatever she's writing, it's all-consuming. The databases? Does she think I'm an idiot? Anger rolls up, rolls through me. It isn't that she's lied to me; it's that she looks more focused and intent than I've been for two years.

As I watch her, my mouth waters. *It isn't fair,* a small, wounded voice says in my head. *But who said life was fair?* I respond. *Who said in life you get to do what you want?* I'm one of the lucky ones—I got to do what I wanted for years and years.

"Can you check these out or should I go to someone else?" A vaguely familiar woman with pursed lips and big, black-framed glasses interrupts my Patricia vigil. She's holding a chunky bestseller and looks annoyed. I could swipe at her, get rid of her, but I look at her and say, "I'm happy to do it." Smiling, opening my hand for the book. She makes a disbelieving sound in the back of her throat, a muted *hmph*, and passes it to me. When I open her account and see the red flag, happiness floods my heart. "Oh," I say, scanning the lines slowly, like a doctor reading a doomed patient's chart. "What? What is it?" She cranes her neck to see my screen. She already knows, though. I can hear it in her voice. "You have a hold on your account. For five overdue books, from months ago. So the fees are . . . significant. Forty-two dollars total," I say, raising my eyebrows. Before I can react, she's reached across the counter to grab the book and clutch it to her chest. Something flares up in me then. That's our book. *Ours.* "That's ridiculous," she says. "I returned those books ages ago. I told Nasrin and she said it was okay to keep checking out books. But if you want me to pay something, fine. Take this." She pulls out a crumpled five-dollar bill and throws it down. It sits between us on the counter; I refuse to pick it up. It doesn't begin to compensate for what she owes—and she looks fairly well-to-do. As well as belligerent and red-faced. Without thinking, I reach for the book. She tries to pull away but I wrap my fingers over the top. "Stop!" she screams. "Stop! You're hurting me!" she yells at the top of her lungs. I give the book a hard yank and manage to free it. The woman stumbles back as I clasp it now to *my* chest, the plastic wrapping cool under my hot hands. She stands there huffing, staring at me, staring at the book. A laugh is about to bubble up out of me right when Yvonne appears. She gives me a look and then ushers the woman to an empty chair, speaking to her gently. The woman blubbers to Yvonne as I stand there, holding my prize.

Nasrin appears and now both of them comfort the woman, giving her a tissue to wipe her face. As I watch them minister to her, something in me yields. They could be nurses on a ward. They look just as caring, just as generous and giving. My grip on the book loosens. Should I join them, help them soothe her? But then Yvonne leaves the woman's side and beckons me into her office with an impatient gesture of her hand.

I hide the book beneath some old papers under the counter. They can pat her back all they want, but I won't have them handing it over.

Seated across from me at her crowded desk, Yvonne

looks at me levelly. Her lips are pressed together, her hands are folded on the desk. Behind her, colorful paintings by local artists crowd the walls, just as they did when I first had my interview. But that happy day feels distant now, unreachable, and a hot flush, followed by a cold chill, go rushing through me. *You could lose this job. Your sanctuary. You idiot.* "What the hell was that?" Yvonne asks, sounding very unlike herself, and a lot like the voice in my head. I try to dredge up cheerful, sanguine Margo, hoping she'll tell Yvonne she's terribly sorry, that it was all a mistake, and then turn it into a joke somehow, but that Margo is paralyzed. "You're normally so patient with the patrons, but lately I've noticed a tendency to overreact, and even lash out," Yvonne says in the silence. I open my mouth to speak, but she holds up a hand. "I know how frustrating it can be out there. I spent twenty years on the floor, before I became director. I miss it, actually." Her eyes look dreamy as she says this. As if she'd trade all her lunch meetings and conferences and fundraisers for a day on the floor, with "the people" again. "I know it can be tough, though. I know how it can wear you down." She gives me a nod and I nod back. We both know I have what it takes—the grit, the patience, the gruff sense of humor. I just lost my way for a moment. Or two. "But what is always required, as I know you know, is CPR: courtesy, patience, respect. I've never had cause to worry about you before, Margo. You've been . . . an outstanding worker. But in recent weeks, a couple of incidents have troubled me. I've seen you really lose your cool. I can't have that out there. I can't have you disrespecting patrons—no matter how trying they may be—in my library."

Her voice has risen, and when she finishes, her lips are set in a grim line. She gives me a cold, disappointed look that makes her resemble one of the hospital administrators I dealt with along the way. Not the one at Spring Hill, but another, earlier one, someone I'd always been able to laugh and chat with. She told me she couldn't ignore the reports from my colleagues, or the incidents of "unusual" patient deaths, even without solid evidence. Her hands were tied, she said, lifting her very free hands in the air. I hated her then. She was cowardly, willing to sack an excellent nurse because of rumors that might tarnish the hospital's reputation. I would never call Yvonne cowardly, but looking at her now, I know she'd stamp out my peaceful little life here like one of my fires if she thought I was hurting *her* library.

"Is everything all right with you, Margo? Are there—is there anything affecting your work?" She's shifted gears, from stern boss to concerned colleague. I force myself to focus, to parade the Margo she knows and loves before her now-sympathetic eyes. I wave my hands at her. "I'm fine," I say. "I've had some trouble sleeping lately. My doctor says it's something to do with my hormone levels. But otherwise I'm fine, and I'm sorry for . . . what's happened lately. I've been short-fused, but I'll work it out. The doctor gave me something that should help." I stare at her earnestly as I say it, and she looks relieved. She looks as if she expected me to say something worse, and I wonder what. "Oh, if you're having trouble sleeping, that can really affect mood, performance, everything! I'm glad you went to your doctor." She seems eager now, so happy to have this easy excuse. I seize the moment. "I'll do better, I guarantee it," I say, rising from my chair and reaching out my hand. She looks taken aback, but she accepts my hand and shakes it, limply. I turn to go.

Another bout of seething rage takes hold of me as I walk back to the circ desk. I was seething in Yvonne's office, too, but I kept it under wraps. I could have clenched her hand hard and pulled her across the desk until our eyeballs touched. I did not. I just saw it in my mind for a moment; now I'm trying to let it go. What I can't let go of is that everything was *fine* here until Patricia showed up with her prying questions and watchful eyes. I was never in danger of losing my job before she came; I never strayed from my soothing routine before she showed me that book. I kept my secret to myself, too, before Patricia. She has deeply unsettled things. Unsettled *me*.

Nasrin is helping a polite, slender man when I rejoin her. I see her eyes flit to me, then look away. She takes her time with his pile of books, clings to him so she won't have to face me. I'm making my scary face, my scowling one; she'll see it in due time. What happened was her fault, too, and she knows it. If she hadn't given that patron a pass, we'd never have tussled. That's why you can't bend rules for people. They'll push you as far as they can—until one or both of you snap.

In the meantime, I take my seat and remove that book the woman fought me for from its hiding place. I glance at the cover. *Saving Adeline*, it's called, by Miriam Gladner. The image is of three cartoon women in profile, walking down a sidewalk. They're caught in midstride, fully in sync, intent on saving Adeline, I suppose. I'm sorry to have risked my job for this nonsense. I dump it on the returns cart and look toward Patricia, obliviously writing away in her bubble. I imagine her scribbling down what happened just now: *Margo looks demented as she snags the woman's book. The woman, startled, stumbles back and cries out, "You're hurting me!" But Margo doesn't care; she's grabbed the book and stands glaring at the woman.*

I should march over to Patricia right now and demand to see that notebook.

But I won't. She'll deny it anyway. And I've promised Yvonne not to make any scenes. It's time to take a deep breath and recover my upbeat self. I lift the corners of my lips to make a go of it.

◆ ◆ ◆

At home, I lower myself heavily into the bath. I've added bath gel tonight, telling myself it's for a treat, when, really, I just can't stand to see my body submerged like a wallowing sea creature. All I can see is a layer of froth—though my toes peek out. I don't mind seeing my toes. I lie there breathing deeply, trying not to replay today's unfortunate encounter but doing it anyway: How I lunged for the book, how the woman stumbled back. And then how I endured Yvonne's shaming and threats like a schoolgirl. I close my eyes to try and shut it all out. I see Merricat standing at the gate—in real life instead of on a book cover. NO TRESPASSING/PRIVATE. She's protecting me, helping me. The skirt of her dress flutters in a warm breeze and she raises her right hand as if to say *Stop* to the villagers. Or maybe just to wave at me. I wave back, lifting my hand from the water and hearing the fat drops hit the surface of my bath.

When I open my eyes, the water has cleared; the bubbles have dissolved. I can see my body, but it doesn't disturb me now. I'm at peace with my body. I feel tenderly toward it. Good, solid body, one that fills the tub, one that carries me through the calendar of days. I smile down at it, magnified underwater. When I notice the tips of my breasts and the rounded hill of my belly pimpling with cold, I pull myself up and out, welcoming the warm towel and the prospect of hot milk and early bed, just as I have a million times before. *A million times before, a million times more.* I say it over and over in my head, feeling sleepy and soothed before I've even had a sip of milk.

♦ ♦ ♦

Wednesday is a quiet day, a good day. I've been good. I've been friendly and laughing Margo, efficient Margo: refilling patrons' printing cards and putting books on hold; finding large-print editions of popular novels and fixing the scanner. Nasrin and I have kept up our usual light banter in between tasks—about the weather, celebrities, local government, and her dog's latest mishaps. I laugh at the story of how her dog gobbled a granola bar and then promptly barfed it back up. Liz is with us, too, and we're getting along. She brings us pumpkin-flavored lattes at lunchtime; Nasrin claps her hands in delight. "The first pumpkin-flavored treat of the season," she exclaims. I smile at her straightforward joy and grope around in my mind for some trace of the anger I felt toward her yesterday; it's gone. She and I are good—she and I are golden.

Despite my good mood, though, I've avoided looking toward the reference desk. I've caught glimpses of Patricia, of course, hunched over her notebook as usual. I wonder if Yvonne might catch her at it and give her a talk. A little warming fire lights inside of me, imagining Patricia chastised like me—flustered, ashamed, and fumbling to explain herself. Yvonne might even fire her. My heart constricts at that, though. I may have been angry yesterday, but I don't want her gone; she's part of us now, here at Carlyle Public Library.

I'm looking tenderly at Patricia, close to tears, when Liz sidles up and blurts, "I'm curious what she does all day, over there." She nods toward Patricia. I feel a wave of revulsion at her nearness and take one step to the side. "She does her job," I say firmly. Liz shrugs, still looking. "I don't see her studying the reference materials or cataloging anything . . . she never *moves.*" *Her hand moves*, I could say defensively. But it wouldn't be much of a defense. "Everything's online now," I tell her instead. "It isn't like the old days, Liz. She's looking at the computer and jotting down notes. That's how the job is done—in this century." Liz lifts her eyebrows but doesn't respond. Usually, she would find a way to flaunt her master's degree and show how much she knows, but she doesn't this time. "She's taking *a lot* of notes, then. A whole book's worth." Liz turns her head and peers at me significantly over her reading glasses; I stare back. Finally, she gives a soft *harumph* and turns away—away from Patricia, too. I didn't like the way Liz said, *A whole book's worth,* as if she, too, knew Patricia's secret. She can't, though. Patricia only confided in me.

◆ ◆ ◆

It's the next day that causes me trouble—and I can't even say why. I'm not angry or disturbed. I've maintained my composure and my friendly efficiency. I've even won a dimpled smile from Yvonne, which feels like a triumph. But then I rest my eyes on a patron, late in the morning. Just a random man whose name I can't recall. He was typing with great energy, but then he slowed, and now his head has started to nod over the keyboard. He does a familiar dance: nods, nods, and then snaps his head back up and groggily resumes his work. I feel amused at first—that's all, just amused—but then I find myself watching him more intently, the way I used to watch certain patients who'd caught my eye. I tune in to the ring of white hair around his head, the right-arm brace he's wearing, the crisp collar of his pale green shirt. I wonder how old he is, if he has family, how healthy he is. How strong is the thread attaching him to life? Is it thick, a muscled cord, or something more like frayed rope? It looks like frayed rope from where I'm sitting. And just thinking *frayed rope* ignites the spark in me that always said: *This one. This woman staring out her window with her hands limp at her sides. This young man with the disfigured face and stuttering heart.* I get lost in the sensation, watching him nod and nod. Suddenly he snaps awake—fully awake—and pushes back his chair to leave. He isn't old and infirm after all—he's middle-aged, stocky, muscular even. I recognize him then: he's the man who burped aloud and said he wouldn't use our bathroom because he valued his life. His little eyes find me and he smirks, breaking the spell. I come fully back to myself, regretful and smarting.

◆　◆　◆

I've found a new spot for my fires, out of sight of Patricia's window: a nice private rectangle of asphalt between the edge of the woods and a dumpster in the back of our parking lot, half-filled with construction debris. It's harder to build the fire there—I have to carry wood from the stand of trees and stack it precisely—but the flames get going eventually. I throw in an old hospital name badge I scrounged from a drawer; I watch *Jane Rivers* shrivel and melt, fold in on herself, and burn down to black.

Good riddance, Jane. Get ahold of yourself, Margo. I watch the fire for a long, long time.

And I follow it up with a good, scalding soak. No bubbles this time; only hot, hot water. When my flesh hits the surface, I remember that original fire, the one that consumed my childhood home. Flames lapping the hem of my nightgown, blistering my little toes. It hurt to hell and back, but I was never one to cry, even then. I stood silently when I made it outside, watching flames leap from every window, straining my ear for screams, though it was far too late for that. When the firemen came, one scooped me up and pinned my head to his chest, but I rolled my eyes as far as I could to the right so I could go on seeing the raging beauty of that fire. It was the first great thing I'd made; I wanted to savor it. Later, at the station, the detective leaned close. *Did you check on your mother and stepdad?* I held his eyes and said, *No.* I wouldn't lie. If he'd come out and asked, *Did you start that fire?* I might have said, *Yes.* But of course he didn't ask. He only nodded and took notes, just like Detective Parson. They love their notes, don't they? What do they think they'll figure out, in all of their scribbled words? The key to the crime? Answers to the mysteries of life? I give a hearty laugh that echoes in the small, humid room, thinking of how Detective Parson's marvelous eyebrows would have lifted if I'd laughed this way in answer to one of his ridiculous questions.

Post-bath, I stroll through my rooms barefoot, enjoying the feel of soft carpet under my feet, pulling down blinds and locking myself in for the night. I feel cozy, cool-headed: safe. I think back on the day, remembering the man I thought was ripe for help. *What if he was? What if his head crashed into the keyboard?* I see him there, drooling. I come up behind him, take his hunched shoulders in my hands. Shake him. He won't wake. I lean down and whisper harshly in his ear. He still doesn't stir, so I pinch his wasted cheek, the papery skin of his arm. I pinch him hard enough to make him scream, but he slumbers on. I place both hands around his neck then, loosely, and tighten them slowly. I look up and see my own distracted, dreaming face in the bathroom mirror. My hands are clasped together, tightening on the nothing between them. I shake them loose and shake myself out of this state. I see my pupils: dark and wide, eating up the blue.

After this, I pace the living room. Back and forth, back and forth, treading the soft carpet. It isn't unpleasant, but I wish I could stop. I haven't done this since my hospital days, since the days when I burned with urges. I know eventually I'll tire myself out; I'll be as sleepy as the man at his keyboard today. I pace so fast the walls blur as I go by.

◆　◆　◆

On Friday morning, after my restless night, I notice things I shouldn't, like the pulse in one woman's neck as I scan her books: *Basic Teachings of the Great Philosophers*; *Buddhism for Beginners*; *Zen Mind, Beginner's Mind*. I watch the spot on her pale flesh and imagine the low, intoxicating beat of blood through her body. It gets louder as I listen, barely raising my eyes. Like I have an ear pressed to her chest. Or a stethoscope.

I distract myself by looking at the reference desk. Patricia is gone. Out sick? No clue. Now that I'm used to seeing her there, the room feels off-kilter without her. It's as if time has moved backward, back to the time before Patricia. And if time can move back that far, can't it carry me back to those earlier days in the hospital? *Don't be ridiculous.* I turn to the calendar behind the circ desk: October 27. Time *hasn't* moved backward. *You're here in the library, you fool. You've built a new life, and you've put the old one behind you. Now go shelve some books.*

Later, I watch a mother hurry to the stacks with two children in tow. When she approaches the desk, the bags under her eyes and the tendrils of frizzed hair around her face tell me she's barely getting by. She won't have time to read the mystery novels she's holding; she doesn't have a life outside of caring for her children. She looks tired, so tired. I long to help her rest, to show her to a bed with clean white sheets and a crisp pillow, in a room with a locking door. I would see her settled, pull the sheet taut, and pat her legs. *Good girl. Let's have a nice rest.* But I don't have a room like that anymore. The bathroom could do. I could steer her downstairs, ease her onto the cool green tile . . .

"Come on, Mom," the older of the two girls says, eyeing me suspiciously. "Good-bye," I say, giving her a little wave, humming inside with the vision I've had.

It builds instead of fades as the minutes pass—the humming, I mean. I feel almost electrified.

A body on the cool green tile. Not Julia's body: a new one. A fresh one. A body I could guide there from the start, and ease into place, and linger over for a languorous while.

◆ ◆ ◆

Friday Guy walks in. The electric current kicks up a notch; it fizzes down every limb and fills my ear. "Huh?" I say to something Nasrin has said. "Your friend is here," she says again, louder this time.

He's wearing a bright red baseball hat to shield his shifting eyes; letting his bare, meaty arms lie along the desk; moving his quick fingers over the keys to call up those naughty sites. He darts his eyes toward me, then away. Toward me, then away. I let him wait. I make myself wait, too, with that buzzing in my ears. Soon I will walk over and whisper something I've never said before. Something I shouldn't say. Something that could alter the course of things. I shouldn't do it but I'm ready to do it, hungry to do it, I can't help doing it, so that's that.

That's that. That's that. It sounds like a heartbeat, like that woman's heartbeat I thought I heard earlier, like Friday Guy's heartbeat, reaching my ears through the general roar.

Friday Guy gives me the most beseeching look. I start to move around the desk.

"Margo?" Patricia says. She's standing there with some-one I don't recognize. Not a patron, I don't think. Just a man—a boring man, blocking my path toward Friday Guy, who is not boring, who always gives me what I want and need. "Margo, this is Dan. My boyfriend?" He gives her a look at the question in her voice. All I can think is: *These two strangers are standing in my way.* I could shout at them, *Move!* But that would be a scene, and I can't have scenes, especially now. I have to move quietly, be careful. "I think I told you— he's visiting from Chicago? I wanted him to see the library and—everyone." I know she means she wanted him to meet *me.* I extract my focus—quickly, painfully—from Friday Guy to muster a smile. "Welcome to Carlyle, Dan. Patricia has been great, really . . . intent on the job." Patricia blushes at what we both know is a lie, but Dan just nods distractedly and gives the room a bored once-over. Why should I be wast-ing my time on this rude person when Friday Guy could stand at any moment, gather his bags, and slip away? The humming and the heartbeat inside me grow so loud I nearly gasp. I look away from these two and latch my eyes back on Friday Guy.

"Excuse me," I say, and add a hasty, "Nice meeting you."

When I reach him, Friday Guy is blatantly watching porn. A naked woman writhing on a naked man's lap, her red lips arched in a pseudo-ecstatic smile. Friday Guy's hands are just inches from his penis, and I'm surprised he isn't rubbing it through the fabric of his pants. His mouth is half-open, his eyes are glazed.

A bright fury rises to the back of my throat. I feel Patricia's eyes on me and I remember Yvonne's warning and *Jane Rivers* burning in the fire and I lean close to pour my heated words in his ear.

He looks up at me, startled, his gray eyes wide, his whole being brimming with relief.

PATRICIA

The Tuesday morning that follows my intense happy hour with Margo proceeds as usual: I dress with care, ironing my hair so that it swings against my shoulders like a dark, shining curtain. I drive the same route that Margo walks, scanning for her on the side of the road, though I know she sets out early and arrives long before I do. Sure enough, I find her at the circ desk on pushing through the library's front door. She calls out, "Morning, Patricia!" then goes about her work. I study her when I can, as discreetly as possible, or I find my eyes drifting her way when I'm in between sentences, searching for words.

Outwardly, nothing has changed about the job; I'm still awash in odd calls throughout the morning: *Can you help me find a place in town to buy celery soda? What's the schedule for the antique car shows happening this weekend? How do glasses work, how do they make you see?* And odd visits, too, like the woman who brings her remote control to the reference desk and asks me to change the batteries. But since learning Margo's identity and deciding to start my novel in earnest, I feel almost saintly with patience and eager to help. When a tall, stooped man interrupts my writing to say he's afraid of his upcoming colonoscopy, I lock eyes with him. Lean toward him. Tell him I haven't had one yet, but that it's good he's doing it. If he has them regularly, I say, the doctor will be able to catch disease early, and probably cure it. I don't bother looking up a medical website or worry about the boundaries of my "role." I just speak to him as I would to a friend, and he thanks me before turning away, clearly relieved.

I sit there glowing once he's gone, not even desperate to grab my notebook and pen, to get back to the narrative flow he interrupted. I let my eyes rest on Margo. She seems cheerful, as usual, chatting with patrons as they hand over their materials, trusting her with their sorrows, secrets, passions, and fears. She learns so much about everyone, just by what they hand her: self-help guides for manic-depressives, books about paying down debt or becoming a millionaire, audiobooks on marital trouble. *Poor souls*, she would say if she could, clucking her tongue over everyone's troubles. Their failings. Their soft spots. Maybe she knows these people, her patrons, even better than her patients. She saw her patients' everything—but a different sort of everything: bodily fluids and body parts; all the stages of sickening, healing, and dying. But her library work might tell her even more.

In spare moments, I Google Jane Rivers and learn that the case is stalled. She seems to have vanished into air. Former coworkers wonder if she's fled to Mexico or Canada, to practice as a private nurse: they "shudder at the thought." But there are no leads; two years have passed. Knowing this gives me a warm, safe feeling inside. No one from her past is after her—or if they are, they're failing miserably. So I'm free to bring the novel's scenes popping to life. Jane in her blue garb, hiking up her pants to climb on a hospital cot. Her large, chafed hands holding a delicate phial to the light, then shaking it. Her raucous laughter filling a small, enclosed break room full of other nurses and a bitter burned-coffee smell. I scramble to get it all down, feeling as if Jane herself were whispering in my ear, telling me all she's seen, felt, and done. I write it sitting at my desk across from Margo and then, when I put the pen down, I sit there massaging my hand, feeling electrified, alive.

Writing about Jane, I revel in the craft.

It was never like this, when I was writing *The Lost Family*—my abandoned book. That was a long slog, with rare moments of inspiration. The title alone came quickly, came to me early, and I clung to it, thinking it was simple yet evocative, but now I see how bland it is. And the book itself, too—so perfectly "coming-of-age." A family's secrets brought to light . . . the ramifications . . . rolling through three generations . . . Boring and baldly imitative, too, of almost every other novel I'd read of multigenerational family life. I should have known when it was so painfully laborious to write. Nothing came to me; I carved it out of some false imaginary realm instead of drawing it from *inside*, letting what was real and raw flow out of me—like I'm doing now. And how quickly it comes! I run my fingers over the hurried scrawl filling a notebook page and know it: *this* book will never be locked in a desk drawer; *this* book, when I'm finished, will come to light. I look up at Margo. Jane Rivers. Tenderness sweeps over me at the sight of her adding a book to the holds shelf. My very own murderous nurse.

I haven't forgotten what that means: that she's *murdered* people. Many people. The thought comes rising up through my generative bliss every so often; I choke it back down.

But it won't stay down, not for good. I'm haunted by the quotes I've read from the victims' relatives: "My mother was the center of our family, the glue that held us together. She wasn't even that sick—and now she's gone!" "Every morning I wake with the horrible knowledge that my son is dead, and I will never see him on this earth again." "She took my great love from me. Killed her. If I could, I'd kill her with my own bare hands." I have read these with a burning, twisting sensation inside. It's sick, sick, what I'm doing. It's morally wrong. I should call Detective Parson and tell him what I know, but instead I go on sitting here, my head brimming with the details of Jane's crimes: How she stole insulin, morphine, and atropine from supply rooms, then injected them into her patients' IV lines. How she skipped from one hospital to the next, once every couple of years. Her employers had known something was wrong; they'd suspected she was causing illness or death, but they'd never turned her in. They couldn't risk their hospitals' reputations—or the lawsuits that would follow. They'd simply moved her on, like the Catholic Church did with its scores of abusive priests, sometimes with glowing reference letters.

I console myself thinking that at least I wasn't a part of *that*: A systemic scandal of epic proportions. A reason for no one to feel safe setting foot in a hospital again.

I'm not anywhere near that bad, that culpable.

And what if I did call Detective Parson and let him lead Margo away in handcuffs? I think of the yawning emptiness at the circ desk. The achingly blank pages in my notebook. And bitter disappointment, my steadfast companion, creeping back. There would be no novel; there would be nothing again. Nothing but this job, which is only tolerable while Jane's story sustains me, while Margo sits nearby.

I'll call Detective Parson when I've finished the book.

Or when I've found an agent and sold it successfully.

Or maybe just on the cusp of the book coming out.

Of course, I couldn't do that. Then he'd read my novel and know what I'd kept to myself. I'd be outed as Margo's accomplice—which might sell books, but I'd be vilified, and possibly imprisoned. So the only scenario for telling Parson is: telling him now. Dropping my pen, closing the notebook, forgetting my hopes for the book. I sit for a moment, imagining that.

After a short, distracted pause, my hand begins to move across the page—slowly at first, then faster, capturing Jane and her setting: the shine on her neat blond hair; how silently she moves into a patient's room at night; how the glow from the machines lights her serious face as she straightens sheets, lifts heads to plump pillows, then leans down close, so close, to her beloved patients. Her special ones.

So much for picking up the phone.

◆ ◆ ◆

During Nasrin's low-key birthday celebration, I spend the time watching Margo perform the simple, basely human act of eating a cookie. I feel like I'm eating a cookie, too, as I gobble up every last detail of her person: her recently touched-up blond roots, the high arch of her neatly plucked brows, the smallness of the cookie in her hand. The studious way she chews, then washes it down not with soda or water but with milk. Milk she produced from a private carton, marked with an "M," in the fridge. She's having cookies and milk, like a child. Her eyes dart to my face and look away. *The Milk-and-Cookies Killer.* I nearly laugh aloud. Who would believe me? Who would believe this incredible scene?

Maybe it's my intent focus on Margo that makes me careless enough to share my own truth.

"You're a writer?" she asks, and I think I hear something more than curiosity in her voice. Suspicion? Fear? Does she somehow know what I've been writing in my notebook? But she can't. I tell her no anyway, and explain exactly why and how I'm not a writer. How I failed at being one and gave up. She doesn't look satisfied—any more than I would be—but Liz's arrival helps me escape before Margo can press me for more.

I keep looking behind me as I walk upstairs, as if Margo could be running after me. *Hey! You're a writer, right? You're a writer!*

Back at my desk I write faster, write more, as if she were breathing down my neck, exclaiming, *You're a writer!* Like a threatening cheer. One that scares me but also eggs me on, increasing my delight as I form each word in blue ink on the page. I fill the page and turn it. That sense I had, of sickening guilt, has long since faded. All that matters is that Margo is with me, alongside me, my terrifying muse. I saw her come up the stairs and resume her seat at the circ desk. She's over there but she's *here*, crucially driving this scene of Jane next to her soon-to-be victim:

> She observes how Alma's prematurely white hair curls and waves around her head in a kind of cloud, how it sets off her smooth olive skin and bright green eyes. Even though she smiles often, Jane can still see her fear: of the twists and turns her sickness may take, of leaving her daughter, of death. Jane's job, she knows, is to swoop in, lifting her spirits the moment she opens the door. Alma chatters to her happily, points out her new bouquet sent from a friend, a vase filled with pink peonies. "It looks like they're celebrating a baby's arrival, doesn't it? Instead of . . ." Her voice trails off. Jane pats her hand and tells her they're lovely, absolutely lovely, and no one deserves them more.

I remember a bouquet of pink peonies my mother received—how luxuriant they were, how their scent filled the hospital room. I realize, then, that I've written my mother into the book—with her bright eyes and prematurely white hair—in place of some anonymous patient. That Jane will creep back some night with her filled syringe or her paper cup of pills and the daughter won't be there—no one will be there—and the disconnected alarms won't sound. Jane will clamber up—

I stop myself there. I should tear out the pages I've written, crumple them up. A sane person would. A *good* person. A good daughter.

So I do, or halfway do: I open my notebook and tear out what I've just written. But at the last moment, I don't crumple the pages up; I fold them in half and slide them into the back of the notebook.

It doesn't stop my mind from working, though. I don't think about my mother, or about how sick it is to imagine Jane as her nurse; I don't think about the real victims who suffered at Jane's hands, either. I think about Jane instead: what she feels, what she wants. Is it power? Does an ice-cold curiosity drive her? Or a furious urge she only half understands?

I give the notebook a push so it scoots across the desk. *Let's put it away*, I tell myself. *Bury it. Lock it in that desk drawer at home and do something else. Something clean and light filled and useful, like being a librarian.*

Right at that moment, two women approach my desk, asking to see our local history room. I fly up out of my chair, startling them with my eagerness to assist. I find the key in one of my drawers and lead them to the room. "Is there a specific area of Carlyle history you're interested in?" The older of the two women tells me they're researching a disastrous bridge collapse from 1929; they're collaborating on a book. I nod my head and ask them more, making interested sounds as they detail the calamity. It's almost soothing to hear about this distant disaster that claimed thirty-nine lives; it seems so quaint, even harmless (though it wasn't), in comparison to my calamitous Jane, who potentially killed over eighty patients, though they'll never be sure. I show them to our stack of old map books and the volumes of town records and leave them, reluctantly, to their work. "Let me know if you need anything else!" I call out, but they only mumble thanks, already engrossed.

Just as I return to my desk, wishing I were needed more, I hear the sound of voices raised in argument. Margo's voice is one of them. Of course. What I see looks like Julia Mather all over again—Margo versus an outraged female patron, though this woman looks younger and robust. At one point she throws a crumpled bill down on the counter between them; Margo doesn't touch it. If I were the patron, I'd be scared by the killing look Margo is giving her. If she is, she doesn't show it; the woman goes on resisting, clutching the book she wants to her chest.

Watch yourself, I think. Not sure which of them I'm talking to.

When Margo reaches out to grab the book, I gasp. I stand there watching, hand over my mouth, as the two jostle for control. "Stop! You're hurting me!" the woman screams, but Margo has won; she's yanked the book from the woman's hands and grips it, looking breathless and mirthful. *Jolly Jane*, I think with a chilly delight. I'm *glad* she got the book. Even as Yvonne comes to the woman's aid and a patron nearby shakes his head in disgust, I can't help feeling Margo's triumph ripple through me.

Yvonne beckons Margo into her office and shuts the door while the patron, sniffling, unburdens herself to Nasrin. *Drama queen*, I think, watching the woman coldly. Margo may have gone too far, but she didn't *hurt* her. Not that I could see.

When Margo emerges from Yvonne's office a little while later, she looks composed. Though she must have been scolded, she doesn't show it; she takes her place behind the circ desk with queenly dignity. I watch her extract the patron's book from somewhere under the counter and examine it with scorn. I think she might chuck it away, but instead she drops it on the returns cart, her blank face revealing nothing.

I have to reach all the way across my desk for my notebook. I can hardly remember why I pushed it away. Now it seems as overly dramatic as that patron's performance. I open right to the back and fish out the folded pages, unfold them, smooth them out, and see where I left off. As I read them, I think, *I haven't committed a crime. I'm only writing fiction; I didn't kill anyone myself, did I? Jane did all of that. I can take my mother out of the story when I revise.* I look over at Margo, returned to her sanguine self. I feel sanguine, too; the blood sings in my veins. I have to *write*. That's all: *write*.

◆   ◆   ◆

It's Thursday evening before I panic about Dan. I should have tidied the apartment and scrubbed the bathroom by now. I tell myself that my busy schedule has prevented me, but that isn't true. After two days spent compulsively writing during work hours—with few interruptions—I've been sinking onto my couch at six to watch brainless TV and eat whatever's at hand: leftover Chinese food, slices of cheese, olives, canned chicken, and crackers. I've had plenty of time to tidy; I just haven't done it. I'm in denial, too, that he'll *actually* be here—in my apartment, invading my space—as of tomorrow.

At least I finished those database recommendations for Yvonne. At the end of the day, I deposited the annotated list in her inbox—a report that might have garnered me an A+ in grad school. I was proud of myself for doing my actual job, and for getting it done before the long weekend. Now, on my return home, I focus on getting everything ready: I dust the shelves, vacuum the floors and rugs, and wipe furniture, surfaces, and appliances down. I polish the windows and mirrors. I wash the sheets and towels, finish folding a pile of laundry, and drive to the store for good bread, a selection of cheese, fruit, and red wine. When I'm done, the place shines. I stare around, feeling increasingly wary of Dan's visit—as if he might pollute this lovely place I've made or drag me out of it and back to Chicago. In my earliest days here, I might have let him. Maybe. Now? Definitely not. I glance at my work bag, which holds the Notebook. The Notebook I *will not touch* from Friday to Sunday, I tell myself with a sigh.

♦ ♦ ♦

When Dan arrives at noon the next day, I take him to Monty's, Carlyle's most popular lunch spot. Soups and salads, quiches and crepes. Nothing surprising, but good, standard fare. We sit in a small booth, surrounded by distinctly Midwestern professionals: men dressed in button-down oxfords and khaki pants, women in somber skirt suits. I'm relieved that it's moderately lively, that there's a buzz in the air. Across from me, Dan looks winningly urban, hard-edged and refined amid the soft suburbanites. I admire his thick, wavy brown hair; his tall, mostly trim frame; and his toothy smile. His subtly stylish outfit. We talk and laugh over our nearly identical Cobb salads (his without tomatoes and egg as usual), and I feel a flush of love, a hard pinch of regret. Why was I so anxious to leave him? I've forgotten the feel of those long midwinter months, cloistered in our small apartment. I've forgotten, too, Dan's passionate interest in his dreary work—which I'm starting to recall, as he talks about it now. Talks and talks. I try to focus, but soon my mind drifts back to the reference desk. Back to my quiet space, to my half-filled notebook. To the story unwinding inside it. Margo's pale, watchful face across the way. Dan comes to a sudden stop, clearly expecting a response, but I haven't heard what he's said, so I don't say anything. We pick at our lettuce leaves in the lengthening silence. Finally, he clears his throat. "What's on the agenda next?" he asks.

"Oh, I was going to show you my library."

He smiles and reaches for my hand. As desirable as he is—or should be—I only feel how humid and heavy his hand is on mine. "*Your* library?" he teases. "Okay, sure. Then I can envision you there, hundreds of miles away, whenever I'm lonely." Pain flits through his eyes, though he keeps his tone light. I give his hand a quick pitying squeeze.

Dan catches my hand in his and swings our arms lightly as we stroll through downtown to the library. We pass the ancient barbershop, the faded awning of the faded drugstore, and the prettied storefront of a new home-décor boutique. Dan doesn't comment or pause to admire anything; neither do I. I'm trying my best not to hustle him along, not to hurry his steps toward the library.

The sky is high and blue today, but I feel it bearing down on me like a low bank of clouds.

The feeling lifts, almost magically, as I let go of Dan's hand to push open the library's front door. I remember the first time I came here: the smell of mold, my low-grade depression, my reluctant acceptance of Yvonne's offer. Everything has changed since then—or I have. I don't smell mold, I don't feel disappointed by the worn furniture or the ragged patrons; I feel buoyant instead, and at home, and I immediately start looking for Margo. First, I see Liz and Nasrin, then an elegant older Black man who sometimes asks me for help finding books—he's one of the few patrons who does. He raises his hand in greeting and I'm thrilled to be recognized; I wave back a little too eagerly. But I never stop scanning for Margo.

There she is. Hands on her hips, staring fixedly at someone by the public computers. "Come on," I say to Dan, like we're late to a show. He's been looking around, lightly praising what he sees. But I know what he thinks about libraries.

He's told me before that he hates the miasma of social welfare and desperation filling the air of even the nicest, newest, most sleekly designed libraries. *Contemporary design doesn't make it any less of a homeless shelter*, he's said before. I've told him, of course, about the library's role in fostering equity, providing a physical and digital space for its diverse community . . . but eventually I see his eyes glaze over, the way mine glaze over when he talks about his job. Libraries are homeless shelters, sure; there's no convincing him other- wise. They're certainly nothing like his bright, blandly deco- rated office on the twenty-first floor, the one that holds him high above and safe from the dingy masses.

When we reach her, I see that Margo is too intent on the one they call "Friday Guy" to pay much attention to Dan or to our conversation. Observing her as we talk, I wonder what Dan sees: a Midwestern, middle-aged cliché, I suppose. A casserole maker, an overweight mother, a faithful attendant of church and state fairs. I imagine, for a moment, telling him the truth. He would never believe it. *And who would?* I think, glancing around the subdued main floor. Even if I did tell Dan, and he did believe me, he still wouldn't get it. He'd go from seeing her as an anonymous frump to seeing her as a crazed killer. There would be no nuance, no shading of gray. But Margo is all gray, all shading; she shifts like the sky from one moment to the next.

"Excuse me," she says now, dismissing us so she can ap- proach Friday Guy. I watch as she leans close to his ear, whis- pering something. Dan nudges me, and while I let him guide me toward the door, my head brims with questions: *Is she scolding him? Threatening him? Promising him something?*

My god, I want to know.

Out on the sidewalk, Dan stretches and yawns. "That was nice," he says, meaninglessly. The nonexistent clouds come pressing down again. It's colder now. I pull my jacket around me and zip it up to my throat.

◆　◆　◆

I sleepwalk through the remaining days, hours, and minutes of my weekend with Dan, though I do my best to hide it. We peruse the aisles of tomatoes and greens at the farmers' market, walk the river trail, have sex with the lights on (though I try to turn them off), make pancakes for breakfast, read the paper . . . It's like we're back in our Chicago apartment, back in our old life—the life I thought I'd shaken off. Dan seems thrilled. Or at least content—even here, in substandard Carlyle. I feel trapped and leaden, and resolve to break things off before he goes. In the meantime, it's an effort to keep my eyes from the clocks and calendars; I'm hungering for Sunday, and for what comes after Sunday, too: my desk, my notebook, and a charged return to Jane Rivers's world.

Early Sunday morning, I roll onto my stomach so Dan can enter me from behind. As I shudder rhythmically against the pillow, I call up the scene we witnessed between Margo and Friday Guy: how she looked at him, leaned over him, and whispered in his ear. I imagine her saying, *I'll take care of you. Ease your burden,* and then meeting him in some dark corner downstairs to slip her hands around his neck. To press her thumbs against his windpipe. As the scene stirs to life, Dan's breath comes faster in my ear. *I'll take care of you. Ease your burden*, repeats in my mind, and soon I'm making sounds I rarely make, letting go the way I never do unless I'm alone in a darkened room. Eventually Dan rolls off and lies beside me, panting and sweaty, grinning. I force myself to smile back. *Want to know what made me come?* Turning my head from his blissful face, I squeeze my eyes shut and tell myself I was building a scene for my book, nothing else. It happened to coincide with a climax unlike any I've had with Dan before. The truth is, of course, that I'm sick. I've been sickened. Jane's story has infected and corrupted me. Now I get off on imagined murder—as Margo probably does in her free time. I shiver and Dan reaches out. "You all right? That was amazing," he says, his whole being glistening. "Really rough and out of control. I loved it. So did you," he says, chuckling. He leans in to kiss me full on the lips as I choke back a wave of revulsion.

◆   ◆   ◆

We say good-bye in the parking lot, by Dan's familiar blue car. I pat it gently on the hood as if it were a pet. I've missed the car, actually. The smell of the dark blue interior and the way it roars too loudly to life at the turn of the key. Dan has been cheerful all morning. The thought crosses my mind that he's cheating on me, back in Chicago, and I feel a surge of happiness. *Go on back to your new girl*, I want to tell him. "This is great," he says, and I'm not sure what he means. "I'm so glad it's easy to drive here. What's a few hours? We could take turns every other weekend." When I'm silent, he falters a little. "Or maybe not every other weekend, but close. Until you figure things out." I don't ask what he means by "figure things out." I *know* what he means; he means until I give up this ridiculous job in this nowhere place and move back to Chicago. He's probably saved my closet space; he thinks I'll return and this will all have been a glitch in the long, continuing story of our love.

"I'm proud of you, though," he says, just as I'm about to do The Right Thing and tell him I'm not coming back, that this was our last hurrah, and wasn't it a nice one? "Proud of you for moving on. Putting that book, and those ideas about who you had to be, behind you. You're all grown up now!" he says, laughing and drawing me close. So close that he can't see my face contort in fury. So close that he can't feel me trembling. I kiss him hard on the lips when he pulls back, my hands pressing the sides of his head.

"Good-bye, Dan," I say. And he gets in the car and drives off with a silly wave.

"Good fucking riddance," I say to his glinting rear window.

I turn around before he's out of sight. Without thinking, I glance up at Margo's patio door. I think I see movement, but the glass is full of glare. I'm going home and I'm going to write. I'll write for the rest of the day if I fucking want. I'll imagine my way through that scene between Margo and Friday Guy; I'll figure it out. I can't walk fast enough up the green stairs.

IV.

A Holiday Feeling

MARGO

I wake Monday morning, squinting, to sunlight. Surely I'm not in my own pitch-dark bedroom? I sit halfway up and look around. My rumpled sheets, my tidy bedside table. The digital clock that reads 7:01. My alarm hasn't gone off as it should, at 6:30, and the curtains are wide open, but I'm home. In bed. Confused. I stretch my arms and yelp in pain. Then a flood of recent memories: Friday Guy's bashful look as he stood at my door last night. The cellophane-wrapped flowers he pushed into my hands. Daises and mums: cheerful, but not too extravagant. The beer he carried, too. How I stood aside to let him in, catching his scent of cheap soap and mild body odor. The soap was winning in the scent war, which meant he must have recently showered. Or bathed. I imagined him up to his chin in bathwater and caught my breath, though he didn't notice—he was looking around. He sat down, fidgeting, on my couch. Clasped and unclasped his hands. Wiped his forehead, ran a hand through his hair. He talked about his search for work, his hope of moving out of the studio over his sister's garage. His words carried toward me in the kitchen, where I carefully prepared his drink and made listening sounds. He fell silent when I carried the drinks out on a plastic tray—his beer in a glass, my ice-cold water.

"You don't drink?" he asked as I sat down beside him on the couch, my left knee lightly touching his right. He sounded tremulous but disappointed, too, and gulped his beer as I shook my head.

"No, I've never had the taste for it. And I don't like to lose control," I added, staring into his eyes. He grinned like the man he'd been when I'd first caught him looking at porn, ornery and amused. He glanced at my chest—more orneriness. Too much. I was disgusted with him but proud, too, that he'd actually come. I'd been so worked up when I'd leaned close to whisper in his ear that I hardly knew what I was saying. *I'll give you what you want, you horny prick*, is what I said, and then I'd told him the details for a made-up rendezvous. *This* rendezvous. But I never thought he'd come; I was shocked to see him on my doorstep last night, vivid bouquet in hand.

But I wasn't so shocked that I wasn't *ready*, of course. Jane was always ready.

His eyelids were drooping—he'd chugged half the beer. Nervous, greedy bastard.

His head lolled—forward, then back. I took the beer from his hands and set it carefully on the table. No need to break a perfectly good glass. He laughed as if I'd said something funny, but I'd said nothing out loud.

He leaned on me as I held him firmly around the waist and led him downstairs, out into the lot. It was late Sunday by then and no one was around; the lights hung, dim, over the rows of cars. We skirted the edge of light, heading for the dark back lot, for that spot by the dumpster I'd found. It was cold out, but I'd remembered my coat. And Friday Guy's beer-soaked blood would keep him warm for as long as it mattered. He was trying to speak—his breath making clouds of hot air—but I shushed him, just as I would have if we'd been at the library. It was cozy, shushing him. He quieted down and nuzzled my neck like a child.

When I got him in place, on the pavement behind the dumpster, I stood up to catch my breath. I wasn't as young as I'd been two years ago. I was out of practice, too. I scanned the rows of dark or blue-lit apartment windows, landing on Patricia's. Her windows were black, as I'd expected they would be. She'd had a long weekend, ferrying that boyfriend of hers around. Still, I half-hoped she'd appear, that I'd see her waving and smiling in the window. Telling me this was right.

But that was silly. I didn't need her telling me it was right. I *knew* it was, down in the pit of me.

"Where are we?" Friday Guy slurred from below. "No-where," I said, and he giggled. I fingered the vial in my pocket, the syringe in my other. Souvenirs I'd kept from my hospital days. I felt a flash of that surety I'd always had as a nurse, moving fluidly from one task to the next. Checking the blood pressure in room 110, making sure 32 had had a bowel movement. Opening the curtains in 16 and getting her to eat something, even pudding. I had been so certain, so secure, just as I was right then, touching that cool glass and plastic in my pockets. It gave me a boost. I looked down with my seasoned professional eye and saw right through him—through his skin and bones and hair—to his absolute core. To his polluted, human, hurting self. He was dozing like a baby.

When I lowered myself down over him, the gravel dug into my knees. This was much less comfortable than the hospital—or even the library bathroom. I gritted my teeth against the pain and leaned close. "Steve," I said. I knew his name—I'd always known it. I shook him and his eyes fluttered open enough for me to pry open the lids. His eyes had rolled back; there was only white.

It was time for the shot.

I wanted to relish the moment—my thighs clenching his middle, my breasts resting on his chest as he lightly snored—but there wasn't time. And there never is, is there? When you want to keep something, to turn it in your hands and examine it: the moment *just before*, the moment *just after*. There is always that ticking of the clock, that hot breath on the back of your neck. *Move it, move along, there are things to do and people are waiting.* There was no one waiting then, of course—we were two souls adrift in a dark and empty universe, breathing together, communing in a way most people never do, out in the ruthless world. I could have lain my head down on him and drifted for a while. I lost track of the pain in my knees and began to feel how I'd felt on those hospital beds. Safe, securely held. But something wasn't right. Something nagged at me, stirred in me. I *wasn't* content. I wanted more.

Time wasn't the problem; the hot breath at my neck was my own. I fumbled in my pockets for the shot and filled the syringe from a half-seated position. It slid right into the skin below his ear.

He gasped awake in seconds. His mouth hung open like he wanted to speak, or scream; he flopped on the ground. I slid my body over his like a weighted blanket, and as he seized, I pinned him, soothed him, and fitted my mouth to his, breathed into his. I found his staring eyes, their black pupils eating the gray of his irises. Bliss rose up in me like a hot fist, spreading through every limb. I rode his body as he seized again, again, then went still. I collapsed over him, spent, breathing hot air into his dead gaping mouth.

After several minutes, I rolled off him and lay looking at the starry sky. Letting hot tears run from the corners of my eyes to the pavement. It had been so long since I'd felt such colossal satisfaction. I started to hum. I hummed a tune that came from my full-to-bursting heart, letting it reverberate through my body and the night air. I was one with the night, one with the air and stars and sky. My body was weightless; it floated next to Steve's.

I feel weightless now, too, coming fully awake, bathing in memories and sunlight. I feel like it just happened moments ago, that I just killed him and the stars brightened as I hummed my tune. I think I hear birdsong out the window and imagine seeing those cardinals and wrens I once invented for Liz. I swing my legs over the edge of the bed and try to stand, but searing pain sends me back down to the mattress. My legs and back burn; the pain sweeps away the birdsong and the square of blue sky I can see through the window.

My body. My body, broken because of *his* body. I hadn't thought about dealing with a *body*.

I'd never had to before. I'd been so spoiled! I'd left my bodies right where they lay in their hospital beds. They were no concern of mine; they belonged to the sour-faced morgue attendants or funeral directors who came to collect them. But Friday Guy belonged to *me*—and not in the silky, ethereal, satisfying way he'd belonged to me for those moments before he died. I stood over him, staring at his slack face, his motionless soft belly, and finally understood. He would be heavy, I realized. He would be hard to move. And where would I move him *to*? I could drag him into the woods—but I had no shovel for burying him. In the end, I could only think to get him into the dumpster and cover him up. I fought back tears of frustration, indignation—*this* was how it had to end? So messy and ugly, and was I strong enough to get it done? I had sometimes carried patients to and from the bath—but that was ages ago and they were generally frail, not meaty bucks like Steve.

I rested my head against the cold metal side of the dumpster and fumed. It wasn't fair, but this was how it was. This was how it was. My breath slowed and deepened. Margo and Jane, they did what needed doing.

With effort, I lugged him onto my back and tried to lift him up and over that way, but I wasn't tall enough—he hit the edge and crumpled back to the ground. Then I stood him up, facing the dumpster, and leaned him against it while bracing my arms around his waist. I lifted him up, up, up, and tried to clear the top. That's when I felt the searing pain in my lower back—but I pushed through. After several tries, it worked. He flopped over and into the dumpster: the *squish* of flesh meeting solid objects.

Once I'd hoisted myself up and into the dumpster, too, I saw him, laid out and facedown against the chunks of concrete and other debris: two-by-fours, squares of tarp, metal rods and panels. I turned him over and straightened his arms at his sides, smoothed his pants and shirt, and then began carving out more of a space for his body: a shallow grave. With my arms and back burning, I cleared debris one piece at a time, aware all the while of how Steve would have loved to see my breasts jiggling as I worked. I would have laughed if I hadn't been so out of breath, so sweaty and focused in my winter coat.

At some point, I came to my senses and removed my coat, hung it over the side. The cold air was bracing.

Once I'd created the shallow pit, I dragged him to it and covered him up. First, with two squares of tarp, then with concrete, rocks, panels, rods, all of it, until I was certain that anyone with an aerial view—whoever that might be—would only see a dumpster full of junk.

Friday Guy. Steve. Released from his squalid life; reduced to junk.

When I clambered out and landed heavily on my feet, feeling yet another spasm in my back, I stood there shivering. Picking up my coat, I envisioned the endless string of empty Friday afternoons now stretching before me. Before *us*. I'd deprived Liz and Nasrin of their Friday fix, too. After a few moments of pitying myself, of pitying the three of us, I stopped with the nonsense and carried myself home, staying carefully out of the light. There was really no need: my neighbors were sleeping. The complex was as dead as my friend in the dumpster.

In the bath I cleaned it all away, everything I'd done. I sent it swirling down the drain where it belonged.

Now I've woken, feeling giddy but sore. There's no getting around it: I have to stand up. The clock's digits have ticked up to 7:23, and work starts at 9:00. I push up from the bed slowly, clutching my back, groaning aloud. My god, I hurt. I hobble to the window and see: not a thing. Only clear blue sky over rows and rows of cars, and the lonely dumpster in back. I exhale loudly, relieved, and begin to move through my usual morning exercises: Reaching up to the ceiling, stretching down to my toes. Lying on my back, holding my knees to my chest, then stretching my legs up into the air. When I roll over to stand, it still hurts, but less. And the giddiness remains. Today will be just like the old days, when my secrets warmed me as I made my rounds. If only I could see my old colleagues today: Donna, Dr. Abdul, that punitive administrator whose name I've forgotten. *Look, I'm still here! You didn't stop me!*

But I can never do this again. I can't. This was it: a special case, a sweet single time. *I don't want to lose what I have here in Carlyle. No, I do not.* (Shaking my head, I discover the aches in my neck.) I have to be satisfied; I've had a nice taste but the nicer thing is my life: the library, my patrons, Liz, Nasrin, and Yvonne. And Patricia, of course. I tell myself I'll let it go, nodding once like I'm sealing a pact. I'll let it go like I let him go, over the lip of the dumpster. I look at the dumpster now, obediently holding my secret. It's nice to have him close. Looking out, I can say, *There's Steve*, as I'm dressing for work, undressing for bed. *There's Steve*, as I watch TV—though that's something I rarely do.

♦   ♦   ♦

I've decided to wear a bright floral dress—it matches my radiant mood. I've taken care with my hair and face so my outside glows, too. The cool air chills my legs on the walk to work, but I hardly feel it. There's a spattering of rain and I've forgotten my umbrella, but I hardly feel that either. When I step into the welcome warmth of the library, tears spring to my eyes: I'm home.

"Look at you!" Liz says when she sees me. Her eyes go wide, like she's seeing something odd. "Special occasion?" she asks. "Nope," I reply, resting a hand on my belly as I've seen pregnant women do. I do feel pregnant this morning: pregnant with what I've done. Liz gives my hand a stricken look, then says, "Okayyyyy." I could laugh in her face, but I hold it back.

As filled with warmth and light as I am, the pain in my body thwarts me as I go about the day. I've tried to hide it, but once, when I rose after sitting for a while, I yelped at the fire that shot through my back and legs. I had to slump back down in my seat and close my eyes. When I opened them, Nasrin was there. Big green eyes blinking in my face. "Are you all right?" she asked, touching my arm. I managed to smile. "I'm fine, dear. Just did some cleaning yesterday and overdid it, I think." She nodded understandingly; offered me aspirin, which I refused; and turned back to her work. Since then, I've been doing my best to suffer quietly and walk as normally as I can, without the limp I've developed. *Hot bath*, I think all day, like a running refrain. *Hot bath*. A hot bath will sort me out.

While Liz and Nasrin have been unwantedly attentive, Patricia hasn't noticed a thing. She's hardly looked up from her notebook all day, and when she has looked up, even looked straight at me, I don't think she's seen me. I made a point, once, of walking by her desk on my way to the stacks. I even went to retrieve a book I didn't need from the reference section: an encyclopedia of world wines. But she never stirred, never said hello or asked me if I needed help. I resent her not looking up, not seeing me in my glorious state. I strut around like a (hobbled) male peacock all day. Once, I laugh so loudly at a patron's feeble joke that *everyone* looks up. Everyone but Patricia.

Plenty of others see me, though, and I see them; I circle the floor, asking patrons at computers if they need any help. Yvonne says we shouldn't do this, that they can come to us if they need to, but I don't mind. I help one woman fill out an online application for public housing; I help a man with long, gray dreads log on to his e-mail. I am patient and kind. I pour my whole being into their problems—large and small. *I will help you*, I say with my every gesture and word. *I will fix you and everything*. The man with the dreads looks up at me with teary eyes. "You did it," he says when his inbox appears. "I don't know how to thank you."

◆　◆　◆

In the gathering dark, I stand on my balcony and look toward the dumpster, toward Steve. There's still a reassuring nothing there. The trees beyond the lot stand quiet guard as my neighbors pull cars into spaces, as lights go on in apartments down the row. As far as I know, no one's missing Steve. The sister he lived with might assume he's gone on a trip, or run off with someone. He could have run off with *me*. I would laugh at this hysterical thought, but I'm so melted from my bath, so temporarily drained of both pain and energy, I can barely move the muscles of my face. But I look toward Steve and wish him well. I thank him for the gift of the other night, and I forgive his body for hurting mine.

◆　◆　◆

Morning comes and I stretch tentatively. The aches remain, but so does my internal buzz—both slightly lessened, but still there. I stand, yawning, and move to my bedroom window. I expect to see that wonderful nothing again, but movement catches my eye. Above the dumpster, something is circling. A large black bird with broad wings: a buzzard. My knees tremble as I watch it circle slowly, marking time.

It's just a bird, I tell myself. I'm sure buzzards have circled our parking lot before. Haven't they? I rack my brain to remember. Even if someone sees, they'll assume it's an animal carcass, won't they? A dead raccoon. A lost cat. I have time.

I'll bring home a shovel and bury him properly tonight. I'm not happy about it, but at least I have a plan. And time. I have time.

I return to the window while towel-drying my hair. Now there are two. Two birds. Two buzzards. Circling.

◆ ◆ ◆

The flush that filled me is gone, long gone. In its place, dark energy zips along my nerves. I'm starving, too. I stood watching the birds too long to have breakfast and pulled on the easiest outfit I could find: tan slacks and a button-down, navy blue blouse I never wear. It's too tight across my chest and on my wrists. I keep twitching my shoulders and fussing with the sleeves, trying to find space where there is none.

"What happened to your sparkle?" Liz asks with a sly little smile, early in the morning. "It's my period," I grumble, and she backs right down. She's fussy, Liz, and doesn't like to talk about bodily things. Even jittery as I am, her discomfort makes me smile.

As the workday progresses, I begin to fall apart: I drop a stack of DVDs that go everywhere, and later, brochures for a series of upcoming lectures for seniors. Kind Nasrin kneels to help me pick them up, but Liz looms over us, clucking her tongue. As if I did it on purpose. As if paper could be damaged by hitting the floor. I keep checking the clock as the day wears on: 10:00, 10:45, 11:13 . . . we creep toward lunch. I eat but have no appetite. I snap at patrons when I shouldn't and ignore them for too long when they come to the desk. In my agitated state, my eyes keep drifting to Patricia. Boring, immersed Patricia, working away at what she once described to me as "not *writing* writing." Bullshit. I know that intense look. That focused, feverish movement of her hand. She's me, stirring Steve's tainted beer. She's me, fingering the needle in my pocket.

I envy her so much, I have to give her a shove.

She looks up distractedly when I reach her desk and clear my throat. Dropping her pen and shutting her notebook, the way she always does. I want to look her in her dreamy eyes and tell her: *We're the same. Gripped by a lifelong passion, grinding our souls against the world's unjust demands.* Or something like that. Patricia doesn't have to bury bodies when she's finished, though.

"How was your big weekend?" I ask, my voice too strident for the question. "It was great. Really great," she says, coloring with the lie. "That's good. He'll be coming back soon, I hope?" I can't remember his name. Dave? Matt? Her color deepens, and she stammers, "Well—he—yeah, sure. He'll be back." I can see how badly she hopes he won't be. All she wants is whatever's in that notebook: no distractions, no visits from the boyfriend, no one standing at her desk making chitchat. "That's nice," I say, and we stare at each other with fixed smiles. "You've been so busy over here." I gesture vaguely toward the desk. My eyes flit to the notebook and she actually spreads her hands over it, shielding it. "Yes, well, there's a lot to do," she says like a lame reproach, a hint to me to *move along.* I stand there for a long moment, staring at the backs of her hands before I go.

When I've returned to the circ desk, I track the quick,

jerky movement of Patricia's hand across the page and envision stealing the notebook. Waiting until she's away from the desk—if ever—grabbing it up and sticking it in my bag. Taking it home and dropping it right into one of my evening fires. Grinning like a witch as it burns down to nothing.

Then what would she do?

That would be fun. But I have other things to tend to.

Right when the day ends, I'll go buy a shovel at the hardware store. I'll get a smaller one, tell the salesman I need it for gardening. I'll bring it home and at night I'll dig a grave in the little woods and drag his corpse on one of the tarps and cover it up and smooth the dirt over the mound and cover that with leaves. I'll be finished then. I'll be able to relax and breathe again. I'll recover my Margo-ness then and get on with my life.

◆　◆　◆

It rears up before me, my beloved, ugly home, as I hump this damn shovel down the sidewalk. There were no small shovels in stock, so I shrugged and told the clerk this one would have to do for my "garden." Now my arms ache so badly I'm nearly in tears, but the sight of home spurs me on. I hoist the shovel up against my chest and hurry forward.

Almost there. Almost there. I repeat it until the edge of the lot comes into view.

And then the flashing lights.

Like at the hospital.

Like at the library, just the other day. Those cherry-red lights, for Julia.

Flashing lights on cars around the dumpster. Police. EMTs. Yellow tape. A group of my neighbors clustered by the building. Others leaning from their balconies and windows to watch.

I want to drop the shovel but I can't. I hold it as naturally as I can, readying my lie: *It's for tending my plot in the community garden.* No one cares about my shovel, though; most of them don't even see me. They're fixated on the flashing red, the gruesome thing the dumpster holds. Some have glasses of wine or beer, like they're standing around at a cocktail party. There's a holiday feeling in the murmur of voices, the mingling crowd.

"It's a body," an elderly neighbor says as I pass her to reach the blue staircase. I nod but say nothing, as if I already knew. "They found someone's body." Her eyes are wide—she's put her hand on my arm. I pat it, then gently remove it.

"That's a shame," I say, my voice quavering, though I manage to smile. "What a terrible shame."

PATRICIA

I pass Margo limping home from work, along the side of the road, carrying something. A long stick-shaped thing. A broom? No, it's a shovel. I turn to stare and twitch the wheel as if I might pull over, but in the end, I drive by. She was so curious, earlier today, about the contents of my notebook. Even though I'm certain she can't know what I'm writing—how could she?—I don't have the energy now for one of our strained conversations. She's only limping a bit, after all, and when our shared building comes into view, I see that she doesn't have much farther to walk. She'll be fine.

I see the flashing lights, the commotion, the crowding on balconies as I'm pulling into my usual parking space. *What the hell?* My heart starts hammering. The police are clustered around that old dumpster in the back lot; they've taped it off and surrounded it with more official vehicles than I've ever seen in this town. The whole police force and EMT squad must have come. I step out of my car and move toward the building, thinking I'll watch, discreetly, from a window or my balcony, when I run into a neighbor from across the hall. "They found a body," he whispers, though it's clearly not a secret. "Right there in the dumpster. Right here in our parking lot. Can you believe it?" He looks almost gleeful, and there's a holiday feeling in the air: neighbors chatting in groups on the sidewalk, some holding drinks. I struggle to remember my neighbor's name in the midst of sudden panic: Jeff or Richard, maybe? *A body.* A body was found in the parking lot of my building. In the parking lot of *Margo's* building. I flash back to her odd behavior over the last two days. I've only noticed now and then, from the corner of my eye, or when I've looked up to take a breather from writing my book. She was manic on Monday, and today she was dour and skittish. She came to my desk, vibrating with interest and intensity, asking about Dan, our weekend, my work. Staring down at my notebook like she wanted to eat it. It was deeply unsettling. And now I've just seen her lugging home a shovel. Would she do that, though? Kill someone, toss him in the dumpster, and then carry a shovel home in plain sight?

Yes, Patricia, she just might.

My arms break out in gooseflesh: *Margo must be responsible for this body in the dumpster.* I glance around as if someone might recognize me as the passive accomplice to murder that I am, and I find that my neighbor, oblivious, is still going on.

"Mila Harris in 23A called it in. She thought it was an animal. A dead animal. She saw the buzzards today—did you see them? Two of them. Great big things," Jeff or Richard says, spreading his arms and flapping them. It should be comical, but it makes me shudder. He notices and drops his arms. "Oh, I know, it's awful, isn't it? A dead animal would have been bad enough, but this? It's just terrible. I just hope it isn't one of our neighbors." He looks pensive for a moment, but then he spots someone newly arrived and leaves me, calling the person's name. I stand alone, scanning the horizon for Margo. She should be arriving soon to the unwelcome sight of police cars and caution tape. I have the urge to warn her, to stop her from coming. But maybe she saw the scene already and turned right back around, dropping her shovel, heading back to the library. She could hide there for a while, until it gets dark and most of the excitement dies down.

I realize then that she might flee again, disappear in the night. My stomach drops at the thought, a moment of vertigo. *Run, but don't run far,* I tell her. *Please.*

I feel claustrophobic down here, among all these people. I climb the green stairs, push open the door to my apartment, and, rather than stand on the balcony itself, I stand behind the floor-length curtain and peer around it, peer out like a guilty person might.

It's the liveliest scene I've encountered since moving to Carlyle. I look down on it hungrily: the silent, flashing red lights; the yellow police tape surrounding the scene; the huge tent they're erecting over the dumpster. And then the people below, most of whom I've never seen before, all gathered and chatting as if this were a Sunday barbecue, not a crime scene.

I'm just thinking of retrieving my notebook and pen from my work bag when I spot her: standing at the edge of the lot, holding the shovel tight to her chest. I can't read her expression from here, but she must be shocked. I'm afraid she'll turn and run, but she strides forward, moving steadily toward the building, toward her particular staircase. My heart thuds with fear. Someone stops her at the base of the stairs, probably to tell her what's happened; Margo says something back and then plods up the blue steps. No one but me seems to have noticed the shovel; why should they? This morbid little festival is far too distracting. Who cares about the lady with the shovel? I can't help feeling a ripple of delight. *She made it*, I think, exhaling into the curtain. I go on watching but my mind is drifting, wondering how she might have done something like this, so different from her hospital murders—and alone. Maybe not easily, but I've witnessed her resourcefulness and grit. The wheels of my writerly mind begin turning, seeing her with her faceless victim. A man? Yes. A man.

She would have brought him home, drugged him, watched him die. I know from my research—and from what I've seen myself—that she relishes the moments just before death. Then what? The body. She would have waited for the darkest part of night, then wrapped it in a rug to take it downstairs, hoping no one would see her, or hear the sound of the body thumping against each step and then dragging along the ground. When she reached the dumpster, she'd have lifted the body up and over. It would have been dreadful, hard labor, and after, she'd have stood there breathing heavily, her mouth expelling clouds of hot air into the cold night. As she walked back home, she would have glanced around nervously, then stolen up the blue stairs.

Did she pause for just a moment and consider ringing my bell? Asking me to help her? I imagine saying, *Yes*. Then gritting my teeth to help her lift him over the rim, to send the stranger's heavy body crashing down.

The details of the scene I missed are brewing in me now. I slide the curtain closed and pull out my notebook and pen. I feel unstoppered, the words spilling onto the page. I'm having that sensation I've had before: of Margo speaking in my ear, telling me what she did and how it felt. How she feels now, in the aftermath. My hands are shaking when I finally put the pen down. I feel like I really did carry and dump the body alongside her, even though she didn't ask and I didn't say yes, and I'm sitting here, snug in my cell, with no blood on my hands and no body in sight. *I'm not guilty*, I tell myself, closing my eyes. *I'm just writing things down. I'm just making things up.*

♦　♦　♦

The next morning at work, I overhear Liz and Nasrin questioning Margo about the body, having seen it on the news. "Isn't that your place?" Nasrin asks, wide-eyed; they don't know that I live there, too, and I hope she won't tell them. "Yes," is all she says. "I thought so. Did you see it? See the body?" Margo gives her a stony look. "No. Of course not," she snaps. "They didn't have it out on display. Don't be so ghoulish." Nasrin draws back, chastened; she and Liz turn away to their tasks.

As the day wears on, I see signs of Margo's general disquiet. She tugs at the wrists and neck of her blouse as if it is too tight and fiddles with her glasses while staring into space. Her eyes dart around the room, too—as if she is looking for someone. Someone who's missing? Or someone who suspects her, like I do?

Maybe it's my lack of sleep from the night before—I stayed up writing, and then stewing, into the wee hours—but when Margo passes by toward the end of the workday, I catch her. I say her name louder than I intended; she looks up, startled. "What a nightmare, right?" I shake my head and watch her try to mirror my doleful expression. "It's so terrible—right on our property!" Her eyes are wide and her lips tremble as if she might cry. Maybe she *is* on the verge of tears—terrified, now, of being found out. "Were you gardening?" I ask with sudden boldness. "I saw you carrying that shovel." Her lips move for a moment without sound. Finally, she manages, "Oh. You saw me? Yes, I was going to work in the garden, but after they found the body . . ." She shakes her head as if too troubled to finish, but her eyes are glinting and hard. A sliver of cold runs through me. I could push her and ask, *What garden? Where is it exactly?* But I'm neither brave nor stupid enough; instead, I backpedal furiously. "I'm sorry," I say with feeling. "What an awful reason to miss your time in the garden!" Margo's eyes soften; she heartily agrees. When she walks away, seemingly satisfied, I take a deep breath and let it come shakily out.

♦　♦　♦

It's Thursday when the detective returns. He's wearing the same black hat and removes it, grandly, as he walks through our doors. I see him before Margo does, then watch her fix him with her gaze. To my surprise—and probably to Margo's, too—he turns toward the reference desk and approaches me, letting his fingers rest lightly on the edge of my desk. "Ms. Delmarco," he says, giving me a slight, gracious nod. I acknowledge him with a smile, my eyes darting to Margo. She's staring intently at the two of us. "Do you mind if I take a seat?" he asks, not really asking my permission, of course. I gesture toward one of the nearby chairs, which he pulls up and perches on across from me. He retrieves his small notebook and pen and sets them on my desk. I'm highly conscious of my own notebook and pen, sitting just to the left of my hand, directly in his line of sight. I feel an urge, like a twitch, to cover it the way I do whenever Margo approaches, but I keep my hands still and fold them together before me. I attempt a smile and try not to give any outward signs of the startled beating of my heart.

"You live at 442 Roadway, correct?" he asks, pen poised above paper. I nod as heat rises to my face—as if merely answering his question reveals my guilt. I feel the words rise in my throat, the words that would end this conversation—and everything else: *Margo, behind you, is the one you're looking for. She killed the person in the dumpster. She killed many others before that, too.* I could keep my face straight and my voice low, and smile at the end, so that Margo would never know. I could do it now and be done with it. Instead, I swallow and wait patiently for his next questions, trying not to clench my hands. Trying to remember to breathe. "I guess I don't need to tell you what happened there yesterday, huh? Terrible thing. You must be upset, to have that right on your—front lawn, as it were." I scramble for words. "It's shocking. I moved from Chicago not too long ago and didn't expect to have things like that happen *here*," I say. "I thought I was coming to a sleepy little town." I try for a slight chuckle, but my voice cracks. Parson simply nods and scribbles notes. I risk looking up to see Margo openly staring, a blank look on her face. Or is it a focused look? Is she straining to hear us? I tell myself she can't possibly hear us, and besides, I've said nothing objectionable. So far. Detective Parson settles in, crossing his right leg over his left and moving through a series of questions that circle closer to the matter at hand—about how long I've lived in the apartment building, how I like working at the library, where I was Sunday and Monday nights, and finally, what I might have seen or heard on those nights. I'm relieved to be able to answer these questions matter-of-factly: I've lived in the apartment for about a month, I enjoy my work, I was home Sunday and Monday nights, I saw and heard nothing.

It was only later that I saw *everything*, of course—but only in my mind, which I transferred to paper. What if I showed him a few key pages from the notebook sitting right by my hand?

"And did you see anything odd or noteworthy on the day they discovered the body? Any neighbors acting . . . weird? Anyone who, I don't know, seemed nervous?" His question catches me off guard. I see Margo so clearly, humping that shovel down the road, coming upon the lights and the chaos, barreling forward with that determined lurch in her step.

"Um," I say, managing to shake my head as I look him in the eye. "No. Everyone was . . . disturbed. But also kind of enjoying the whole thing, you know? Or not enjoying, per se, that's the wrong word, but it did seem that people were worked up. Excited, even. In a bad way, of course." I'm not sure what Detective Parson makes of this word salad of mine, but he's writing things down in his notebook. "But no one in particular you remember? I realize you may not know any names, since you're new to the area. You do know Ms. Finch, though, don't you? One of your neighbors." He smiles then and tips his head back slightly to indicate her. She's distracted right now by the presence of a patron. I could take this brief window of safety, of freedom from the weight of her gaze, and tell him: *She came home carrying a shovel. She told me she planned to work in the garden, which doesn't exist, as far as I know.* Instead, I say, "Yes, I know Margo, of course. But I don't remember seeing her that day. Outside of work, I mean." The detective stares at me for a long moment, then bends to his notebook, moves his pen. He abruptly stands. "Thank you, Ms. Delmarco. I appreciate the help. I hope your building recovers from all this fuss before long." He flashes his bright white smile, lifts the hand holding his hat in a kind of salute, and turns away.

I watch the detective's back as he stands behind the patron blocking Margo, waiting his turn. He has excellent posture and looks as if he could comfortably wait all day. When the patron finally leaves, he approaches Margo with his hand extended, and she takes it. Their conversation is lost to me, just as my conversation with Parson must have been lost to her; the detective leans close and speaks softly. All I can do is watch Margo's face, her frozen smile. Their exchange lasts only a minute or two. When the detective leaves, Margo stalks into the office, comes out with her coat and purse, and barks something at Nasrin. Then she hustles down the back stairs.

I panic when she's gone. Is this it? Is she being arrested? I approach Nasrin, now alone at the desk. "What happened? What did he say?" I ask, trying to master the tremor in my voice. "He wanted to question her down at the station," Nasrin says, but when she sees what must be my stricken look, she shakes her head kindly. "She isn't in trouble. He kept saying that. But because she knew the man and she lives at the place—" I stop her with a raised hand. "Knew him?" I ask. Detective Parson didn't mention anything to me about the victim's identity, and I didn't have the clarity of mind to ask.

Nasrin leans close, lowers her voice, and looks around. "It was Friday Guy," she says. "Friday Guy is dead. It was his body in the dumpster."

I don't remember much of anything else. I think Nasrin asked me about my own talk with the detective, and I gave her vague, noncommittal answers. I may have admitted that I live in Margo's apartment complex, too—there was no way around it. She may have been shocked. Now, somehow, I'm back at my desk, but I don't remember walking here, or sitting down, or placing my hands carefully, unmoving, on the keyboard.

Friday Guy. I helped Margo kill him by saying nothing, by doing nothing. I had the chance, a few minutes ago, to put things right by telling Parson, but I chose not to. I chose to support the killer of a library patron. The killer of patients. The muse for my book. But it doesn't matter, does it? The police seem to have figured it out for themselves. Despite Nasrin's assurances, I doubt Parson would have invited Margo to the station if she weren't a serious suspect. They may keep her there. Imprison her. This could be it, the end.

A wave of despair washes over me then: *Margo, captured. Margo, gone.* I stare dolefully at my notebook; I can't imagine opening it again, with her missing.

◆　◆　◆

But on Friday morning, she's back.

She comes breezing through the door in a bright red-and-white-patterned dress, wearing lipstick to match. I'm stunned, but I feel a euphoric lift, too. *She's back! She's free!* I watch her flit around, as joyful as she was before the body was found, feeling joyful myself. She catches me staring and walks right over. "Morning, Patricia." Her eyes drift to my notebook, which I've covered with my hands. "Everything all right?" she asks, as if *I* were the one who'd been to the station. "Y-yes," I say after a moment. "And you? Is everything . . . all right with you?" Margo's red-lipped mouth goes wide. "Oh yes," she says. "Everything is a-okay. Thank you for asking." She goes on hovering before me, her eyes pinning me in place. "Did you have a nice day yesterday?" I realize exactly what she's asking: *What did Detective Parson say to you? What did you tell him about me?* If she's here, and looking this gleeful, it's clear they couldn't hold her, but it's also clear that she wants to know what I might have revealed. Something about her nursing past? Or the shovel? Or her odd interactions with Friday Guy? I scramble to appease her.

"Oh, it was weird, that detective coming in," I say, holding her gaze as steadily as I can. "Asking questions about the day they found Fri—the body."

She arches her eyebrows in what looks like an imitation of Parson himself. "He asked me about it, too," she says, leaning close to me. "How I found out, how I felt when I found out, how well I knew him, that sort of thing. Is that what he asked you?" I nod and say yes, though of course he didn't ask any of those things. "Anything else?" she prods.

It isn't like Margo to be so transparently pushy; beneath her cheerful veneer, she must be feeling desperate. At least a little. Even if she's walking free, the cloud of suspicion still hangs over her. Parson could return; he could call her back. He could have found new evidence at the site or located a witness. I won't add to her agitation by answering truthfully. "Not much, really," I say, shrugging. "It's weird that he would bring you down to the station to ask you the same questions he asked me here, isn't it?" I add, innocently as I can.

A flash of fury lights her blue eyes. "Waste of my damn time," she spits. "As if I'd have anything to do with something like that! As if either one of us would. They should be looking for the real culprit, not wasting their time questioning us upstanding librarians, right?" She chuckles heartily then, but it's forced and too loud, even for her. I try to chuckle along with her but my cheeks ache with the effort. I pray it won't go on for long.

V.

Word After Word After Glorious Word

MARGO

I hadn't meant to get into the nitty-gritty of my talk with Parson when I spoke to Patricia. I'd only meant to have a bright, simple chat for a few minutes, to show her how buoyant I was, how unbothered by that interlude at the station. I also wanted to know what she'd told him; I knew she hadn't mentioned seeing me with the shovel, because Parson hadn't asked about it. But *someone* told him about my relationship with Steve—if one could call it that. That could have been anyone, though: Liz, who spared me a curt nod and a mumbled hello to welcome me back; Nasrin, whose eyes fluttered like a child's when I caught her staring; or Yvonne, the one who told the police about my argument with Julia Mather. Patricia could have done it, too. Patricia, whose eyes followed me from the moment I opened the door, who can't have missed my Merricat-inspired dress, who drew me to her like a magnet. Well, regardless of who blabbed, I'm here, showing them all that I may have visited a police station yesterday, but I've returned now, free and easy as any one of them.

I told Detective Parson everything he wanted to hear—that the dead man was a mild nuisance, and that I dealt with him firmly because no one else would. *I was always professional*, I told him, *even though the man was constantly looking at disturbing images online. And looking at parts of my body, too! He was very troubled, you know. It isn't incredibly surprising that things ended the way they did for him.* Detective Parson bobbed his head in understanding, taking notes. So many notes. I liked that he was taking down every word, because every word I said was unassailable. I sat there looking dignified, I'm sure, with my shoulders back and my head held high. The kind of person who was disgusted by the kind of person Steve was. The kind of person who should never have to deal with someone like that. That's what the detective must have been thinking. He was embarrassed to have called me in. Apologetic. And then he said, softly, *It's strange, isn't it? That you had complicated relationships with two patrons who recently died, one at the library, the other, ostensibly, in the parking lot of your home?* I could have startled at this, or stumbled, but I looked him squarely in the eye and gave him a rueful smile. The same smile I gave to my neighbor when she told me about the body. *It is strange, Detective. I've found that life itself is strange, and that these coincidences only prove it. It's tragic, though,* I said, shaking my head slowly. The detective shook his head, too, and said, *I agree.* Not long afterward, he let me go. He said he may have more questions for me another time, but that was all for now; he seemed satisfied, and so was I—to walk out through the same door I'd entered, sure of my doom, and find myself out in the cool, bright day, free and unscathed.

It was after three p.m. when I left. I thought of the person, whoever she was, who was responsible for the time I'd just spent in that ugly concrete box, that place for criminals and outcasts. I wasn't going to dwell on it, but I decided to skip the rest of the workday. Let them stew, let them wonder what had happened to Margo. Let them wonder if they'd gotten her locked up. I knew how dramatic it would be when I returned Friday morning, lighthearted and blithe, like nothing bad had ever happened, like nothing ever could.

Not to me, at least.

After a substantial bath, I stood at my window, staring at the dumpster, feeling the pre-bath woman creeping back. Or not exactly the pre-bath woman, but a bereft woman, a wounded and vulnerable woman. They'd removed Steve's body two days ago, but the yellow tape remained, fluttering in the breeze. I watched it dance and remembered what it felt like before, when Steve was still there, only feet from where I stood. I hated those damn birds, and that meddling neighbor, for causing his removal. He could have stayed there, under those rocks, for a long, long time. It was just as I'd told the detective, in a roundabout way: losing Steve was a tragic thing.

I wasn't afraid of discovery. I could tell Detective Parson didn't suspect me, not really. I could tell he considered me a lead in the absence of other leads, or a way to cover every base. How funny it would have been if I'd blurted out:

Actually, I've killed more people than anyone knows. This one was just an afterthought, something to tide me over for a while.

I could shout it out now—in the midst of the library's quiet, in the face of my coworkers' stares, their creeping suspicions. They look at me now like the villagers looked at Constance and Merricat. *Why is she here, so cheerful and brightly dressed, after such a humiliation?* They think I should be somber, repentant, dressed in muted tones—beige and gray, maybe. But I won't be ashamed; I won't hide my vibrant light.

The clock moves close to two thirty, the time when Steve used to come through our door. I don't mean to wait for him, but I do. I know he won't come slouching in, carrying his stupid bags, consuming his porn, ever again. But I go on watching. My eyes sting with tears as the minutes go ticking past his time. I feel the others' eyes on me, but when I look up and around, at close to three, Patricia is the only one in sight—at her desk, writing, not paying me any mind. Her black hair gleaming under the light. The library is full of patrons right now—sitting at tables with open laptops, roaming the fiction aisles, browsing the "Fall into a Book" display—but none of them seem to need me. They must need *something*, though; I'll have to ask. I'm about to make the rounds when Yvonne steps out of her office and says, "Margo, could you come in here for a moment?" My heart stutters in my chest, but I manage to nod and smile. When I follow her in, she asks me to close the door.

"You've had a tumultuous time recently, haven't you?" she asks when we're both settled in chairs. Her voice is low and smooth, her look sympathetic, her hands folded before her on the desk. The reasonable administrator, the caring, observant boss. She reminds me of the clueless social worker they assigned to my case after my childhood home burned down. All queasy faux-warmth and lollipops, trying to bribe the truth out of me. Which she never did.

"I'm not sure what you mean," I say, keeping my voice even.

"I just mean—with the recent events. Two patrons lost in a short while. One of them found near your home. Interest from the police." She lists them all, staring at me as if I were slow. I give a light shrug and prepare to say something along the lines of what I said to Detective Parson—*Life is strange, loss is tragic*—but before I can, Yvonne clears her throat, reaches out to straighten some papers on her incredibly tidy desk, and continues. "It's just that—I've noticed some erratic behavior on the floor—as we discussed not long ago." She levels a look at me. I realize my underarms are damp and wonder if she can see stains spreading. "I think you should take some time off, maybe two weeks or so, and sort things out." "There's nothing to sort out," I retort, then regret it. I've scared her, I see; the knuckles on her clasped hands are whitening. "I can tell the recent events have been getting to you, and I think you need time off. You need to take a break from work for a little while." More firmly now, more commanding. She doesn't smile; she doesn't say, *And your job will be right here waiting for you when you get back.* Or *I'm not sure how we'll manage without you for even such a short time!* No, I know what she's doing: gently, sneakily forcing me out. At the end of two weeks, after I've twiddled my thumbs at home, I'll get a call, or an e-mail, and Yvonne will tell me that I can't come back. That I'm not so indispensable after all. That the library is no longer my second home, my safe retreat. My eyes start to fill with tears, and Yvonne reaches across to pat my hand. I have to fight the urge not to pull it back or slap her with it. "You deserve some downtime, anyway. You never take vacations. You're never sick. Go home and take care of yourself for a while." I want to tell her that *this* is where I care for myself, *this* is where I heal, but she wouldn't understand. She's done with me, she's said the last word. I try to rise from the chair, but feel gravity and my still-sore muscles weighing me down. I push harder, putting my hands flat on Yvonne's desk, and eventually manage to stand. "You can leave early today, if you like," Yvonne says in her softest voice.

I look in her eyes, so full of what seems to be genuine concern, and shake my head. "I'll stay until the day is done." She nods and puts her hands in place on her computer keyboard, ready to move on. She looks relieved now that our little talk is over. I walk out with the burden she's shifted to me, as heavy as dead Steve, as hard as heaving him into the dumpster.

When I leave her office, I look at Patricia, the ghost who goes on writing. She was writing before, and she's still writing now, after what Yvonne just did to me. She's untouched by the cruelty of the world, absorbed in that notebook of hers, writing and writing. A metallic taste fills my mouth; burning hot tears fill my eyes: I'm being kicked out. Kicked out of my *life*. This might be just a "job" to Patricia—one she routinely neglects—but for me it's much more. My haven, my community, my life. And now, two incidental deaths and I'm done? A couple of justified outbursts and that's it? I fight the urge to tip back my head and howl.

As I watch, Patricia puts down her pen and stretches her arms in the air, then brings her left wrist to her right hand and rubs it. She looks as sated as someone wiping her mouth after a succulent feast. Suddenly, she stands up. She comes right toward me, wearing that dreamy, satisfied smile. "Hi," she says, but she keeps walking. She's just passing me on her way to the bathroom—the place where we truly met, where we truly connected. It feels like eons ago, and she's back to being a stranger. Everything I don't know about her is contained in that notebook of hers—it must be. I can see it from here, closed on a pen but left in plain sight. I stand stock-still, listening to the sound of her retreating footsteps, then I speed across the carpet to Reference, reach out, and pluck her notebook from the desk. The pen falls to my feet. Before I bend to retrieve it, I open to a random page:

> . . . when she punctured the skin of the patient's neck with her needle she gave a deep sigh. It was a sigh of relief and release, something close to ecstasy. But not quite. Ecstasy would come soon, when she would clamber on top of the woman and lie astride her, put her face close to hers, breathe in her musty breath, and watch her die.

I freeze for a moment, absorbing the words. Rereading them. Then I flip frantically through the notebook, finding references to "M," descriptions of my face and figure and even outfits I've worn in recent weeks. I read a scene about "M" standing over a fire in the woods, burning evidence, that makes my blood run cold. I knew she might have seen me lighting fires, but this reads as if she hid in the woods and watched me. I read another part that describes Friday Guy's murder and the disposal of his body; some details are off, but the essence of what happened is there, again almost as if she'd been watching. But she can't have been. She must have imagined it all, but imagined it around a hard kernel of fact.

She knows about me. About Jane.

I stand, leaving the pen where it is, and fling the notebook away from me. It scoots across the desk and lands on the floor. I look behind me, but Patricia isn't there. Wild-eyed, I run around the desk and pick up the notebook, clutch it to my chest. I walk back to Circulation as calmly as I can. I know just the hiding place: a drawer of old lecture flyers and book-group meeting notices that should have been cleaned out weeks ago. But the mess serves me well; I slide the notebook inside, under all the paper. Close the drawer. If there were a lock, I'd lock it. Then I stand, breathing hard, with my shaking hands poised over the keyboard, staring at the black screen.

She knows. She's writing about me. About who and what I really am. I hate myself for letting my guard down, for telling her I was a nurse, for telling her even that sanitized version of my troubles at the hospital. About my sudden departure. It must have sounded suspicious to her, so she did a Google search, or something more sophisticated. She's a reference librarian, after all. Like a fool, I told an expert researcher some truths about my life!

Certainty seeps coldly into me: I have to leave. I might have survived Yvonne's "two weeks' rest"; I might have returned from it and been welcomed back into the fold. But now, knowing what Patricia knows and what she's *doing* with what she knows, I'll have to make a swift and total departure. And undergo yet another painful reinvention in another new place.

I clench my hands together and fight the urge to bring them up, to cover my face and sob. I don't want to go. I want to stay here in Carlyle and go on being Margo Finch, I want to spend every day working under these high ceilings and over this beige carpet, helping those who straggle in, in need of my careful, loving assistance. This is my sacred place. My home. I'm at home being Margo. She's ruined it. Patricia has ruined it.

I'm about to let my tears of furious sorrow fall when I hear her steps on the stairs. I collect myself and grab up the phone. "Yes, yes, that's right. You have two more weeks," I say to the ringtone. "No, you don't have to renew. Just enjoy the book. Oh, it's a series, is it?" I say, pressing the phone to my ear and watching Patricia. Watching her reach her desk. Watching her look around like a lunatic. All around, even under the desk, and in all the drawers. "Oh, that sounds wonderful! Very romantic. I'll have to give that a try." Patricia is still looking, her face a troubled mask. Then a terrified mask. I chuckle into the phone. "You take care, too, dear," I say. "I'll see you here soon." Though I won't. I won't.

Unless.

Patricia looks up, looks right at me, as if she's heard the notion forming in my mind.

PATRICIA

I come back from the bathroom, still in a dreamlike state, caught up in the morbid scene I was writing about Jane. I'm eager to sit down and get back to it. I want to dig into it, dig deeper, expand on the details. Ideas and images have bloomed in my mind since I left the desk. I have to remember to take breaks now and then, to walk around, to let things percolate. It's good for the book—to let it breathe while my mind rests. To come back, refreshed. Not that I need refreshing; I'm an underground spring that's been tapped: spurting out, spurting up. Word after word after glorious word.

I reach my desk and first notice the pen on the floor before it. That's odd. I thought I'd tucked it in the notebook. As I stoop to pick it up, I glimpse the empty space where my notebook should be. But it must be here. I run around the desk and grope through the piles of folders and papers, rustle through every drawer, scan the carpet all around, all around: Nothing. Nowhere. My notebook is gone. I have nowhere else to look, so I look over at Margo. She's been on the phone and is just hanging up now. She smiles contentedly as I approach, quaking with nerves at the thought of asking her my question. About my missing notebook. My book. About *her*. "Margo, hi. Have you seen anyone over by my desk? I'm—missing something." Her lips form a pitying O. "I'm so sorry to hear that! I hope it isn't your purse, or something else valuable?" "No, no, I keep my purse in the office. It's just a—a notebook." Her face doesn't change, but I think I see a mean, amused glimmer in her eye. It's gone in a flash; I might have imagined it. "Your notebook? You mean the one you scribble your . . . work notes in?" For the first time, I wonder: Did *she* take it? Is she hiding it somewhere? Did she *read* it? Oh god. Oh no. I start to choke a little, then have a small coughing fit. I can still hear Margo speaking through it, though. "I'm sorry to hear that, Patricia," she says. The soul of sympathy. Murderous Margo. "I didn't see anyone over there, and I've been sitting here the whole time. Are you sure you haven't misplaced it somewhere?" She gestures all around the main floor, as if I could have left it anywhere: in the stacks, at one of the computers, on the magazine rack. As if I were that careless, that out of my rational mind.

"No," I manage.

"That's a shame," Margo says as I walk away. "Such a terrible shame."

MARGO

I watch Patricia wander the main floor like a lost chickadee. With her shoulders slumped, her clothes hanging loose on her skinny frame. She's nothing like the glamorous, sleek bird that strutted through the door all those weeks ago, reeking of urban sophistication and her recent master's degree. Too good for the reference desk, too good for all of us!

Liz and Nasrin return from shelving books, deep in conversation. ". . . and my son is planning to bring his new girlfriend to our house for Thanksgiving. We're all very nervous about meeting her," Liz says. Nasrin is listening, making sympathetic sounds, reassuring her that everything will be fine. The girlfriend will be lovely, the turkey and Liz's signature sides will be a success. They hardly notice me, and I hear them only faintly, like the babbling of a distant creek. Their faint presence soothes me, but my eyes are fixed, fixed on Patricia.

She's returned to her desk and sits there, forlorn, her eyes and hands unable to stop roaming, rifling through stacks of papers she's already rifled through, opening drawers she's already opened, checking the dark recesses of empty cabinets. Finally, she looks up. When she does, I'm ready. I've pulled the notebook out and am holding it up, just below my chin, so that if the others happen to see, they won't think much of it. They'll only see one of those black-and-white marbled composition books. They'll assume it's some student's forgotten homework or an old records book from before our digitized time. But when Patricia sees it, it's different: she rears back in her chair and twists her mouth. Like she's seeing a ghost.

Or some kind of monster—like the one in these pages of hers.

I stand up slowly, still holding her eyes. I move toward the stairs. "You aren't leaving now, are you?" Liz asks, startling me. She knows, of course she knows, about my two-week "break." She suspects, I'm sure, that I was *encouraged* or even *forced* to take the break, and that I'm trying to slink off now to nurse my sorrows at home.

"No, I'm not leaving," I say as evenly as I can. "I'm just running downstairs to the ladies' room." Both she and Nasrin smile pityingly, as if already bidding me good-bye.

I take the stairs two at a time—brushing by a startled patron on the way. I have things to do before Patricia catches up with me. Downstairs, I search through the kitchen drawers and grab what I need. Then I follow the dimly lit hall to the heart of the old stacks, the huge shadowy room filled with shelves and shelves of our oldest, most delicate books. *The rarest part of our collection*, Yvonne told me with pride when she gave me my first-day tour. I've never liked this dreary old crypt, so far from the everyday bustle. But I need its gloomy remoteness today.

PATRICIA

Walking quickly down the stairs, I remember how it looked: my notebook in Margo's big hand. Her eyes glittering above it, her mouth a grim line. It felt brutal, seeing her holding my book. And knowing she had read it. Knowing that she knew that I *knew*, knowing she wouldn't tolerate my knowing. When I passed Liz and Nasrin, I thought of whispering the truth. I thought of pulling Yvonne from her office, too. But in that time, what would Margo do to my book? I thought of all the lines, all the pages I'd filled, of the narrative I'd built, of the words that had flowed from me like water.

I even thought of Jane—my Jane. Of how I'd sculpted her so lovingly on each page, made her live and breathe: my own beautiful monster.

So I passed them in silence, waving at Liz as if to say, *I'm off to the bathroom*, but she didn't look up. She may not have seen me pass by. I'm like a ghost to those two. If I don't come back, will they notice? Not for a long, long time.

I step into the first-floor hallway, hesitant at first. I go from door to door, pulling each one open quickly, but each time I find myself peering into empty rooms. She's not in the kitchen or the bathroom. Either one is too public, isn't it? There's only one viable choice: the old stacks.

I push open the heavy metal doors and stand for a moment in the near-total darkness, my knees trembling. I worry that they'll buckle. After a moment, a light clicks on down the row.

"Margo?" I call, as if she'd answer, *Over here!* As if we were meeting for coffee. But I know it's Margo who's triggered the light. I turn toward it, feeling intensely that I should sprint back through the doors and run upstairs, run outside, run screaming for help.

Then I smell smoke and hear the light crackle of fire. I don't run away; I run toward it.

MARGO

I could laugh at her look of horrified surprise. As the flames begin to leap and play, I want to tell her: *This is more real than anything you've done, anything you've made in this notebook of yours, the one I'm hanging over the little trash can fire.* Her eyes are fixed on the notebook; I'm not sure that if I spoke, she would even hear me. "Please don't do this," she says. As if I had her baby by the arm, as if I were dangling it over the flames as it screamed. No sound from the notebook, though—or from Patricia, either. I like seeing her tremble as the fire just laps the bottom edge of the notebook. Just begins to catch. I lower it to tease her.

"Please. I know I shouldn't have—written about you. I'll stop writing about you. I'll—just give me the notebook!" she screeches, and stretches out a hand. It's sad, really, that she cares so much about a bundle of paper, ink, and glue. I've spent my life caring for real human beings, and she's spent hers caring for dead words written on paper from dead trees.

No one's even *seen* her words; they mean nothing outside of these flammable pages. "Please," she says again as the bottom of the notebook smolders. "Please. I told that detective nothing. I haven't told anyone anything—and I never will. I'll keep your secrets. Just—give me the book."

I have no intention of giving her the book. I have no intention of letting her live, to keep what she knows a secret or not. I simply can't risk it. I don't have access to my usual tools, of course, but the sharp blade of a kitchen knife is grazing my thigh. It will be messy, which I don't like, but the fire will take care of all that. I've disabled the alarms, so there will be time. Time for it to build and catch and burn everything down to melted flesh and bone, or down to nothing. Only black lumps of books, and other black lumps that can't be identified.

I only worry that the fire will rage out of control and burn our library right to the ground—all because of her, because of what I've had to do to keep her quiet. It could be for the best, though. The building is old and we've needed a renovation for years—we just haven't been able to afford it. Hasn't Yvonne said that many times? Wouldn't insurance kick in, in the case of a fire? That would be a marvel. A real gift—Patricia's last. If we rebuilt, Yvonne would forget all about my "break." She would need me too much. I see it now, me in my T-shirt and jeans, elbow-to-elbow with Liz and Nasrin and even some of our patrons, rebuilding the library brick by brick, stone by stone. We would sweat and toil in the sun, then relish our brown-bag lunches in that shady spot under the cherry tree. I'd be so fulfilled by such good, honest work. I wouldn't need any distractions—not for a good long while.

My vision is hazy when I look at Patricia again. I'm grateful to her now, my eyes blinking back tears—though it may be the smoke. "Okay, I'll give it to you," I say, nodding and holding out the notebook. She starts to move. One baby step. Then another.

PATRICIA

I lunge forward, reaching out with one hand to grab the notebook, reaching out with the other to stab my letter opener into Margo's neck. I realize, in that second, that she must have been the one to put it in my pencil cup all those weeks ago, when she prepared my desk. When she wiped the surface clean, and emptied out the drawer, and filled the cup so carefully, so lovingly, with everything I might need. Including a letter opener. And I *did* need it; I needed it for protection when I followed her downstairs. I needed it most when I saw her grope in her pocket for what I knew must be a weapon. A knife? A filled syringe? And now that useful letter opener sticks from her throat. Blood spilling out around it. I step back as she clutches at the wound, sinks to her knees, and then crumples to the floor. I kneel near her, but not too near, holding the smoking but no longer smoldering notebook to my chest, staring at her face as it spasms, feeling the roar and heat of fire at my back but not moving, just watching her face, watching her eyes in particular, as they flutter and stare, as the black of her pupils creeps outward to consume the blue.

It's beautiful. Profound. The most profound moment of my life. I watched my mother die, too, but it wasn't like this—it wasn't something I'd done with my own hand. *I made this*, I think, and it fills me with awe. I hug my notebook closer. It feels suddenly heavier, as if plumped with extra pages.

Margo's eyes go staring and still. I expect to feel panicked, bereft, but I don't. I have what I need.

Good-bye, Jane. Good-bye, Margo.

Reluctantly, I pull the letter opener from her neck—like unplugging a leak. The blood glugs out. I watch with fascination, without revulsion, as it pools on the floor. Then I turn and see that the whole aisle behind me is raging, on fire. Creeping closer every second. The trash can tipped over and rolled during our struggle, during my leap toward her through the air, and then the fire spread easily, catching the old books and pamphlets lining the shelves. The whole room will be on fire soon. The whole floor. The whole building, even. I take one last look at Margo, then leave her there, running up the aisle and down another to the metal doors. Even in the midst of the fire, even after what I've done, even blood-spattered and coughing from the billowing smoke, I'm calm. Centered. Utterly sure of myself.

In the bathroom, I splash my face with water, wash my hands, polish my glasses, and wash and dry the letter opener until it gleams. I look for telltale spots or splashes of red on my clothes and find none—I know they're there, but they're masked by my black silk top and slacks. And while I do all this—wipe and wash and preen—my salvaged notebook sits beside the sink, with only its bottom edge singed. I can't believe my luck. It wasn't luck, though, was it? It was effort. It was *action*. I *did* something. I lunged forward and grasped what matters—and it's sitting there, all of it, intact.

Before I leave, I study my face carefully in the mirror—all the while thinking of the progress of the fire, of the absence of the sound of alarms, of those old books burning, burning, the heat building in that room. My face is blank, pristine. My eyes dark and dewy with life. I turn to look at the last stall, the stall where I first truly met Margo, where she showed me what she was—though I didn't understand at the time—and when I blink, I can almost see her there, entwined with Julia Mather.

I pick up my notebook, push open the door, and run upstairs as if I've been running since I left the stacks, screaming, "Fire! Fire!"

PATRICIA

We stand on the sidewalk, staring at the building, watching smoke unfurl from the lower windows. The firefighters have long since run in, and some have run back out, faces red and smeared with ash, telling us the whole basement floor is on fire, it's moving up, it could engulf the building. They're doing what they can, but: all of that paper, all of those books. Those faulty alarms that never went off. I tell Yvonne, Liz, and Nasrin that no, I didn't see Margo downstairs; I was in the bathroom, but she wasn't there. And now she isn't *here*. My coworkers exchange looks of doom, looks of certain death. They express hope that she's run out the back and gone home, though that doesn't sound like Margo, and no one can reach her.

I managed to replace my letter opener in the pencil cup on my desk, and because all trace of what happened will be destroyed by fire, I can almost imagine that I'm innocent, that Margo simply wandered down to the stacks and was caught by the raging flames of a freak electrical fire. That's what everyone will believe—even Detective Parson, when he hears about the untimely death of his primary suspect. He won't be sorrowful, though, the way we are, he won't sob the way I do at the thought of her caught like that and burned to death. Liz and Nasrin lean on each other, openly weeping. Yvonne sits on the ground, alone, in total shock.

It isn't just Margo they're grieving, of course, but the building, too. Their stately old library, soon to be a smoldering shell. The patrons are scattered along the sidewalk, some looking troubled and scared, some wiping their eyes like us. Something in me wells up as I stand there watching them, clutching my notebook to my chest. These are people I know, people who need help. And no one is helping them, are they? With Margo gone. I set my notebook down on the grass, and I approach them one by one, comforting them with words but also placing my hands on their shoulders, arms, and backs. Telling them it will be all right. They'll put out the fire. We'll have the damage repaired. Or we'll start over. We'll rebuild from the ground up, we'll replace our collection, we'll start a new life. An engaged life. A caring life. A life intertwined with other lives. It will be wonderful. They only stare in response. Shell-shocked, the poor souls. As I make my rounds, I can't help glancing at my notebook now and then, unscathed and full of story—but not the whole story, not yet—waiting patiently in the grass.

Acknowledgments

Many thanks to . . .

Chris Clemans, my superb and stalwart agent, for his feedback, enthusiasm, and all-around invaluable support.

Danielle Dieterich, my hard-working, brilliant editor, whose astute notes made this a better book, and to Sally Kim, for loving the book first.

The entire Putnam team, for making this novel a real and beautiful object in the world, and then putting it into readers' hands. Special thanks to Kristen Bianco, Brennin Cummings, Meg Drislane, Marie Finamore, Eric Fuentecilla, Ivan Held, Emily Leopold, Christopher Lin, Ashley McClay, Aja Pollock, Elke Sigal, and Alexis Welby.

Jason Richman, who beautifully manages the Hollywood side of things.

My smart, dedicated, funny, and fun-loving coworkers at South Orange Public Library, including Lindita Cani and Keisha Miller, who welcomed me warmly when I first walked through the door. I'm especially grateful to Michael Pucci, who told me a True Library Story that planted a seed in my mind, to Brent Shelley, who helped with a crucial (criminal) technical detail, and to Nancy Chiller Janow, who acts as my chief librarian-publicist.

Criminal, the podcast that introduced me to "Jolly Jane" Toppan, and the books that helped me develop my own Margo/Jane: *Fatal*, by Harold Schechter, and *The Good Nurse*, by Charles Graeber.

My local writers' groups—GM and LLLL—for all the friendship, joy, commiseration, and support.

Marcia LeBeau, owner of The Write Space, the quiet oasis where I wrote and revised much of this novel.

My friends, near and far, and especially to my first readers, for their keen insights and endless encouragement: Mona Awad, Courtney Brkic, Camille Guthrie, Amelia Kahaney, Kim Kassnove, Margaret Lewis, Corey Mead, and Karen Mead.

My parents, by birth and marriage, who are wonderfully supportive.

Corey and Caleb, my constants, my everyday companions. How lucky I am to have you.